D1571954

THIRTEEN

NOVELS

Green Lights are Blue
Sounds of a Drunken Summer
The Borrower
Encores for a Dilettante
The Autobiography of Cassandra,
Princess & Prophetess of Troy
Positions with White Roses

COLLECTIONS

Thirteen
Nightschool for Saints

VERSE

Mirrors for Small Beasts

TRANSLATIONS

Narcissus & Goldmund
Herman Hesse

Law and Order
Claude Ollier

Speculations about Jacob
Uwe Johnson

Obstacles
Reinhard Lettau

[with Bruce Benderson]
Event
Philippe Sollers

THIRTEEN
S T O R I E S

Ursule Molinaro

McPherson & Company

Published by McPherson & Company, P.O. Box 1126, Kingston, New York,
12401. Designed by Bruce R. McPherson. Typeset in Times Roman by Delmas
Typography. The paper is acid-free to ensure permanence. First edition.
1 3 5 7 9 10 8 6 4 2   1989 1990 199

This book has been published with assistance from the literature programs of
the New York State Council on the Arts and the National Endowment for the
Arts, a federal agency.

Library of Congress Cataloging-in-Publication Data

Molinaro, Ursule.
    Thirteen : stories / Ursule Molinaro.
        p.   cm.
    ISBN 0-929701-02-X : $16.00 — ISBN 0-929701-01-1 (pbk.) : $9.00
    I. Title   II. Title: 13.
PS3525.02152T48   1989
813'.54—dc19

ACKNOWLEDGMENTS
"Rumors/Murky Haloes" and "Shadowplay on Snow" originally were published
as *Bastards: Footnotes to History* in the Treacle Press Story Series, copyright
© 1979 Ursule Molinaro. "Sweet Cheat of Freedom" appeared first in *New
American Review 12*, 1971, and later in Top Stories chapbook #16, copyright
© 1971, 1983 Ursule Molinaro. "The Cyclotaur" was included in the Fiction
Collective anthology *American Made* under the title "Apocalyptic Flirtation,"
copyright © 1986 Ursule Molinaro. In addition, the author gratefully thanks the
editors and publishers of the following magazines where other stories were
published first in slightly different versions: *Bennington Review, Benzene, Between C & D, Caprice* (formerly *Redstart*), *Denver Quarterly, Hawaii Literary
Arts, New Directions, and New Virginia Review.*

CONTENTS

THIRTEEN

A Late-Summer Stranger
to Herself

SHE TRUTHFULLY FELT THAT the story she was telling   for the third time; the feeling growing more truthful with each telling   was really not her own. That she hadn't been there when it happened. That she'd been out of town when it happened. On a well-deserved summer vacation. That it had happened to another late-summer woman in another unairconditioned apartment, on the seventh floor, on the Upper West Side. Which the other woman had decided to clean   thoroughly; even her book shelves   before the summer was up. Before she went back to school. Back to teaching English, for the first time in more than ten years. Trying to earn her own living again, for the first time in more than ten years. Since her divorce.

Another woman whose late-summer body looked better without clothes. Who was plump & full-breasted like a Renoir nude. & never quite sure of what to wear. & with what?

Who felt that the unsure skirts & blouses & dresses & coats & occasional hats she imposed upon her better-nude-looking body were distortions of her true self, designed for hermaphroditic Modiglianis. Grotesquely unbecoming disguises in which one faced a world of supermarkets. & classrooms.

Or sat in the over-airconditioned twilight of a late-summer cocktail lounge, catty-cornered by the wide-nostriled headmaster of an underpaying New York private school. Who'd been

9

the only one liberal-minded enough to disregard the more-than-ten-year-marriage interruption in her teaching career.

Who had a   perhaps chronic   skin irritation that made his wide nostrils & upper lip glow purple in the over-airconditioned twilight. Above his listening smile.

Who had a bony-elegant wife who wrote monthly horoscope columns & cast natal charts that earned more money than a liberal-minded private school headmaster. & made her better-nude-looking self   & perhaps also the listening/smiling purple-glowing husband   feel dowdy. At a loss for something to talk about, during this informal get-better-acquainted meeting. Over cocktails.

Which prompted her to tell the totally irrelevant late-summer story of a woman she'd never met. Who was the neighbor of a friend of a friend . . .

Telling it   for the third time since it happened: two days ago   as though it had not really happened to her. The way a girl "in trouble" asks for a certain doctor's name & address & price for "a friend of a friend in trouble."

Watching her smiling listeners' faces for a reaction. For their judgment of a woman who had cleaned her unairconditioned apartment in the nude.

Who had forgotten that she had no clothes on   that's what the neighbor of the friend of her friend had claimed when the doorbell rang.

She'd been standing on a hassock, washing out her book shelves, & stepped down & walked to the door & opened it.

& had stood at the reclosed door, & talked with the young man who had rung her bell. Who was her ex-husband's nephew. Whom she hadn't seen since before her divorce. Whom she'd always liked. & liked to talk to.

Who didn't know that she had become his ex-aunt.

Which she'd proceeded to tell him, with many details, standing at the door against which he was leaning. Listening to her with what had seemed unusual politeness. Making her wonder if this was another one of the alienating effects of her divorce.

Which she'd been experiencing from the most unexpected quarters. Old friends who apologized for not inviting her to their traditional dinner parties because she had no escort, & might feel out of place among the other married couples . . .

Before it occurred to her that her ex-nephew might simply feel hot & sticky, standing there in her dusty, unairconditioned apartment. & she'd gone to the kitchen to get a bottle of white wine from the refrigerator. & had reached up for two glasses in the creaky cupboard above the sink. & had caught the reflection of her naked body-profile in the mirror across from the cupboard.

& had frozen in her reaching position. & asked herself what to do that would be the least embarrassing to herself and to her   over-polite   nephew.

Slip into a robe, & return to the livingroom & apologize?

Or go back to the door as she was. Either as though she hadn't seen herself & realized that she was naked, or else as though being naked while cleaning an unairconditioned apartment on a hot summer day was the most natural thing in the world.

Which might make her ex-nephew become still more polite. & wonder how to take his quickest possible leave from a woman who had perhaps lost her mind in the process of becoming his ex-aunt.

Meanwhile she'd begun to open the bottle. Mechanically. Still unsure of what to do. Casting unsure glances at herself in the kitchen mirror. When her ex-nephew had come into the kitchen & asked if he could be of any help. Because he'd heard the cork pop.

& the woman had handed him one glass & the bottle. & had preceded him into the living room. Where they'd sat down on two hassocks facing each other, because the couch & the chairs were piled high with the books she'd taken out of their shelves.

& they'd drunk the wine. & talked about the subjects her ex-nephew intended to major in, after he went back to school that fall. & after they'd finished the bottle, the ex-nephew had

stood up. & said good-bye. & she'd let him out. & had climbed
back up on one of the two hassocks & gone back to her shelf-
cleaning.

& neither the woman nor her nephew had mentioned or
alluded to the woman's nakedness.

For which the bony-elegant private school headmaster's
wife was sure she could offer an astrological explanation. If she
were told the naked woman's sign. & preferably also the ex-
nephew's sign . . .

Which had the sound of a trap being set. Baiting one's
private-school-headmaster-husband's future English teacher   a
recent divorcee   with the curiosity everyone had about one's
fate. About the development of one's relationship with one's
ex-nephew, for instance. To make her admit that she & no other
was that irrelevantly naked late-summer woman.

Whose behavior had obviously been influenced by one
of the four phases of the moon. That ruled most women's behavior. Since the moon ruled their menses. . . .

Did they know that it was a medically acknowledged fact
that women-suicides almost invariably occurred at the beginning
of their menstrual period. In other words: Under the influence of
the moon . . .

But there was just one small point which intrigued the
bony-elegant wife. & that was whether or not the naked woman
had known that it was her ex-nephew who'd rung her bell?

Or would she have opened the door to anyone? To the
mailman? To a woman neighbor, maybe?

Which was the question she'd been asking herself for the
last two days. & was still truthfully unable to answer herself.

She'd been expecting her ex-nephew who had called her
the evening before. But who hadn't said when exactly he was
coming to see her.

She raised her shoulders. Hesitantly. Saying truthfully

that she had no idea. That she didn't know what the strange naked woman had or hadn't known.

While the wide-nostriled school headmaster's private leg came angling for hers around the cocktail table leg. While he drew a wide-smiling comparison between the heat-prompted shooting of the Arab by Camus' Stranger & the late-summer conduct of the   perhaps equally heat-estranged   naked woman.

Whom he pictured as a full-blown peony. Standing there by her door, across from a fully clothed young man.

Both she & his wife were obviously aware that the flower's name peony was derived from peon. Peasant. A full-blown peasant rose cleaning her book shelves . . .

To which she nodded & smiled. While she disentangled her leg. Carefully casual, under the sidelong smile of the bony-elegant wife beside her. Hoping that her disentangling would seem casual. An unconscious shifting of her position, for greater sitting ease.

As she'd done twice before. On the two previous occasions when she had related the same incident. To two very old friends. Also as though it had happened to a strange other woman.

When she'd also been propositioned by a leg of each of the two very old friends. Whom she'd never known to be flirtatious with her in the past.

On whose good or bad graces she did not depend for her new job.

Whose smiling faces she'd also watched. Closely. For a judgment of her late-summer early-divorcee behavior. For a clue from which to deduce if they thought her "strange."

& if they thought her ex-nephew would come back to see her.

Remote Control

MRS. FEATHERGILL IS WATCHING Mrs. Moreno destroy herself.
It has become a one-hour slot in Mrs. Feathergill's mornings.
From 11:00 to noon.

It's not that she wishes Mrs. Moreno ill. She barely
knows the woman, except for an occasional Good Afternoon
when they happen to check their mailboxes at the same time. A
Hello, how are you? if they happen to pass carts in the supermarket.

Nor is Mrs. Feathergill trying to redeem her own marriage
by comparison with what is bound to happen to Mrs. Moreno.
—Any day now: you don't have to be a mathematician
to add $2 + 2$ together.—

But watching a soap progress in your neighbor's livingroom, across eight feet of gravel yard & a low wire fence, is
more involving than watching the same thing in your own livingroom on your TV.   —With a less unexpected cast, or the
sponsor would throw the show off the air.—

It makes Mrs. Feathergill feel that she could change the
script, if she wanted to. That she could stop the story just before
the climax, & save her reckless neighbor for future mailbox/
supermarket encounters.

Which Mrs. Feathergill has no intention of doing. She

14

believes that Mrs. Moreno   anybody   has the right to self-destruct. Although she has never formulated her belief. To herself, or to others.

Were she to formulate it   —tonight, at the dinner table, for instance—   her husband Horace Feathergill, a prominent professor of mathematics at the local college, might not be able to swallow the spear of asparagus vinaigrette he has just brought to his mouth. & her fourteen-year-old daughter Heather, a computer genius at the local high school, would seek her father's near-sighted, faded-blue eyes, to exchange their glassed-in look of tolerance: two near-sighted Nordic intellectuals, humoring this plump, dark-haired little woman who feeds them, & buys their clothes, & keeps them comfortable. Their wife & mother, whom they expect to believe mostly in what you can eat, & wear, & live in.

Most of the time Mrs. Feathergill doesn't mind being one of a kind in a household of three. A Hispanic living between two Nordics. Who tower above her also on the map. At least in the Western hemisphere where they happen to be living. On Chinese maps North is at the bottom.

Most of the time Mrs. Feathergill organizes the lives of the other two without thinking about their   or her   otherness.

Without thinking about a time   —a different time, before the birth of Heather, before Prof. Dr. Feathergill became a professor, after becoming a doctor; when she was still the appliance buyer for the local department store, supporting a graduate-student husband who awed her with his brilliance.

Who used to press her dark, wild-haired head against his heart   —its location coinciding with the top of her head— telling her how wonderful she was. How efficient. Brilliant in her own dark little ways. What good taste she had. (Also in the choice of her mate?) Before her awe subsided. & his heart retreated behind the prominent round stomach that made him look like a pregnant telephone pole.

These thoughts of otherness & different times have begun

to occur to Mrs. Feathergill only since she began watching Mrs. Moreno self-destruct.

After she had the revelation that the Law of Opposites was ruling her household & the Morenos. Who suddenly appeared to her like a mirror image of her own group of three. The exact reverse.

First of all, the two wives & mothers don't look like the name they married. Mrs. Moreno is as tall   for a woman as Horace Feathergill is for a man. She, too, is a telephone pole, although not a pregnant one. At least not yet. Her self-destruction may not reach that point. & she, too, has faded, almost lashless blue eyes behind thick glasses, & mist-colored hair. To which she seemed to pay little attention, until recently.

Prof. Dr. Feathergill & Mrs. Moreno could easily be taken for brother & sister.

They would definitely be taken for the plausible couple, at a faculty party. To which the Morenos happened to have been invited because Mrs. Moreno used to teach mathematics at the local highschool.   —Which still sends her students in need of tutoring.

& Mrs. Feathergill & Mr. Moreno would be taken for the other plausible couple.   —Looking out of place in a room guest-filled with Ph.D.s.

Mr. Moreno owns a hardware store downtown.

The Morenos' fourteen-year-old son is tall & mist-blond, like his mother.   —With whom he may also trade looks of dinner-table tolerance for the dark uneducated other in their group of three, his doctorate-less hardware-store-owning father.

If the faculty party included children   as faculty parties often do   the Moreno son would probably be taken for Heather's brother.   —They're usually taken for brother & sister by the schoolbus drivers who pick both of them up at the end of their street.

Mrs. Feathergill wonders if the distribution of light & dark   tall & stocky   education &   —& taste in her own household will be affected by what is happening in the mirror household next door.

Which she started watching one mid-morning in January, when she happened to look out her kitchen window to check the weather against the report on the radio she keeps in her kitchen, & happened to see Mrs. Moreno sitting on the couch in her livingroom next to a teenage boy with his face in a schoolbook.

The Morenos have no curtains at their livingroom windows, & there was a standing lamp lit beside the boy. Who must be one of the needy students the local highschool keeps sending to Mrs. Moreno for tutoring. A boy of fourteen, or maybe fifteen, with a Hispanic complexion.

Mrs. Feathergill would have gone back to doing whatever she'd been about to do. She has busy mornings, & is not a nosy person. What stopped her was a gesture the boy made: without lifting his face from his schoolbook he slowly reached for one of Mrs. Moreno's hands & placed it between his thighs.

Rooting Mrs. Feathergill behind the red-&-white-checkered curtains in her kitchen.

For what felt like several minutes she stared at Mrs. Moreno's Nordic wrist protruding from the boy's thighs. Until the hand finally pulled itself upward in a lazy motion. & free. & pointed to something in the book.

Which the boy quickly closed, again trapping her hand. He was smiling up into her inclined face.

There followed what looked like an animated conversation. With smiles & headshakes, & nodded frowns, which ended in a butterfly kiss on the top of the boy's head.

Both straightened up on the couch. Mrs. Moreno was now holding the book to the boy's face. He seemed to repeat what she was saying to him. But after a while his head slowly traveled toward hers. Followed by his cheek slowly traveling toward her cheek. Followed by his thigh. The length of his leg.

For the next thirty minutes Mrs. Feathergill watched Mrs. Moreno & the Hispanic-looking boy sit melted into teach other on the couch, staring into the book. & she never saw them turn a page.

Then the lesson must have been over. Mrs. Moreno abruptly stood up, & reluctantly the boy did also. They left the livingroom.

A few minutes later Mrs. Moreno reappeared. She lay down on her couch, with her head at the spot where the boy had sat. She was smiling up at the ceiling, stretching her legs.

It is Mrs. Moreno's smile that assures Mrs. Feathergill that she is watching a scenario of imminent self-destruction.

Some mornings she wonders if Mrs. Moreno & her Hispanic-looking student feel watched   —By her Nordic conscience. By the Great God Pan. By a group of highschool friends comparing Spanish flies.—   Highlighted as they are, like a professional stage set, by the standing lamp at the end of the couch. But perhaps their individual needs are exclusive of the rest of the world. Perhaps even of each other: Mrs. Moreno wishing to stretch the boy's desire, & he wishing to get rid of it.

Some mornings Mrs. Moreno wears a housegown to teach her lesson. Of deep-blue Oriental silk, with a slit up one leg. She is barefoot, & plays a lot with her toes.

On other mornings she wears a strict black suit, better cut than anything Mrs. Feathergill has seen her wear to the mailbox or the supermarket. She wears it with glittering black-&-silver spike-heeled pumps. Even her misty hair has been recut. Revitalized.

Mrs. Feathergill thinks of her dying mother   how good her mother had looked, suddenly, the week before she died
as she watches Mrs. Moreno teach her Hispanic-looking student.

When his nose is in the book, her Nordic hands alight on random parts of his clothes like absent-minded butterflies. When he reaches for them, she gently but firmly holds the book to his face.

Any day now; any day.

Unless Mrs. Feathergill is watching the secret of Mrs. Moreno's successful tutoring method. Which keeps the local

highschool sending her a continuous flow of needy students.
Perhaps this is how she leads her students on to their graduation.

Perhaps the stage set, the professional lighting, the melting of bodies on the couch have been going on for years of
mornings, & Mrs. Feathergill never happened to look into her
neighbor's uncurtained livingroom window before that mid-
morning in mid-January, when she happened to check on the
weather.

A winter storm   dramatic weather of any season
often precipitates intimacy: two startled bodies seeking shelter
in each other. On her livingroom couch Mrs. Moreno's bunched-
up kimono rises & falls like a silken sea above her drowning
Hispanic student.

A winter storm is also a reason for closing schools. Which
is being announced over Mrs. Feathergill's kitchen radio.

The announcement that the local highschool is sending its
students home at 11:00 a.m. vaguely penetrates her consciousness as she stands watching the thickening of the plot.

She vaguely thinks that the closing of the highschool
means that her daughter Heather will be coming home any minute.

& will want lunch.

She vaguely thinks that the left-over London broil in the
icebox will make a good sandwich.

The thought of Heather storming into the kitchen abruptly
dissipates her vagueness: if Heather sees what she is watching—

Which the home-coming Moreno son will walk in on,
after Heather & he get off the bus.

There may be time to stop the tide of the silken sea with
a neighborly phone call. To rewrite the script at the last minute
& give her private morning soap an inconclusive   impunitively
immoral   ending. To save it, perhaps, for a few more immoral
sequels. But she stands glued, watching the sublime concentra-
tion of her two actors cued by their fate.

Sounds of her daughter stomping the snow off her boots

at the door send her flying to the phone in the bedroom. It takes a couple of fast breaths to find the Morenos' number. Hardware store: no—residence. She dials, & listens to several rings. Finally, Mr. Moreno's voice comes on, taped, urging the caller to leave name, number, & a brief message. She hangs up.

Hurrying to the foyer to steer her daughter clear of the kitchen, she thinks that Mr. Moreno has a forceful voice.

AC-DC

[for Bruce Benderson, with love]

SHE ISN'T SURE IF it's a shot she hears, or the backfiring of a truck.

Before she sees two bare bony legs groping down the fire escape outside her bedroom window. In freezing April drizzle. Followed by tight buttocks clad in leopard undershorts. Followed by an unbuttoned white shirt, & a tight white face under a punk hair cut: a crest of orange bristles sticking up from an otherwise shaved head.

She opens her window & pulls the half-naked figure inside. Relocking her window.

He doesn't resist, except with his eyes: Why is she doing this?

He lets her shove him toward the livingroom. Like an object: she thinks: used to being picked up & put down. His naked feet slur traceless across her naked livingroom floor. She shoves him toward the fireplace. Crawl up the flue: she says to him.

Huh? He stands looking at her, his eyes searching her face: What does she want from him?

They turned the heat off a week ago: she says: Just hang in there until it's over.

Outside the livingroom window on the street side, sirens scream closer, converging on her building. He frowns at her, his

21

eyes contracting to brilliant black dots, then hoists himself up into the sooty brick shaft. His toes push against the sides of the fireplace & out of sight.

Why is she doing this?

She walks to the livingroom window & counts: nine police cars. From which spill: sixteen policemen of varying sizes   some with axes   who disappear into her main entrance. One car with two policemen remains sitting at the curb.

Her bells rings. She goes to press the buzzer, wondering what she'll do if the cold-numbed object lets go & falls at their feet.

She opens her door & stands leaning against the inner frame.

The retired highschool teacher in the apartment below hers is asking what type of criminal they're looking for. She doesn't hear their answer; if they give an answer. Only the retired highschool teacher's retired voice, saying that: he's glad he's retired. They're living in terrible times when a teacher can't turn his back on a class to write something on the blackboard.

A sea of upturned police faces is surging up the stairs. Yes: she says truthfully: Yes, I saw somebody groping down the fire escape.

Why is she doing this?

She's a reasonable-sounding woman, dressed in reasonable clothes: clean jeans & a black turtleneck sweater. Her typewriter is still running   in her bedroom, where she works. She'd obviously been typing when she saw whomever they're looking for. If whoever she saw   & pulled inside   is who they're looking for. For whatever reason. She doesn't tell them that whoever she saw & pulled inside is half-naked, hanging inside the flue above her fireplace in leopard undershorts.

Four policemen have followed her into her bedroom/workroom & are nudging her to open the window. Faster. It sticks sometimes: she says; but then hurriedly complies when she sees one of them raise an ax.

Two policemen start running down the fire escape. Two

others start running up toward the roof. & almost collide with
two more who are climbing out through the bedroom window of
the couple upstairs.

Who aren't home at this hour   —The policemen must
have broken down their door.—   Who don't come home until
around 4:30–5:00 o'clock. The husband usually half an hour
ahead of the wife.

Who squeaks like a mouse when they make love. Almost
the instant she walks into the upstairs apartment. & the satisfied
husband gurgles like a stopped-up kitchen sink.

He should be coming home just about now.

Although . . .   it now occurs to her that she heard
something up there before she heard what she's now sure was a
shot. She now wishes that she hadn't concentrated quite so hard
on "The Infections of the Inner Ear" which she's translating for
a medical publication. The deadline for the "Inner Ear" is 9:00
a.m. tomorrow. & she still has more than half to go. She now
wishes that she'd listened before inviting what might be a half-
naked murderer to hide in her flue.

She may of course be hiding the intended murder victim,
who managed to escape half naked.

He certainly looked like a victim, out there on her fire
escape. Which is why she felt prompted to pull him inside. Her
philosophy   borrowed from Simone Weil, the Jewish saint of
WW II   requires that she throw her weight, though it be slight,
onto the lighter scale.

On which she now finds herself in the company of a
punk-object on the run from authority. For want of a more original direction to his life. A half-naked faddist, who probably
ignores the history behind the fashion on which he's elaborating
with orange bristles & leopard underwear.

Although, even if he did know all about it, he wouldn't
be the first unimaginative drop-out to be in love with images of

totalitarian discipline. Nor the first victim to get a kick out of wearing the clothes of his jailers.

The rest of his aberrant imitation-Nazi costume is probably lying in the absent couple's apartment upstairs.

Where she now hears stomping & scurrying. A metal object thudding to the floor. Slow, heavy voices berating a high-pitched whine.

An ambulance has pulled up outside the main entrance. Her door is still open. As is her bedroom window.

Which the last of the four returning policemen considerately pulls down shut behind him. Telling her that: it's chilly out there. Unseasonably chilly for April. Is their landlord still giving them heat?

She shakes her head, her throat constricting, & escorts them into the hall. They tell her: not to worry. They'll be keeping an eye on the place. They press a card into her hand with an emergency number to call in case she sees somebody out there again.

The retired highschool teacher's voice is coming up the stairs, talking about the terrible neighborhood they live in. His face brightens as he catches sight of her, standing in her open door.

He considers her the only other intellectual in their building, & tries to trap her into conversations every time he meets her in the hall downstairs, on her way in or on her way out. Almost every time she goes in or out. He either watches for her to come home from his livingroom window, or else he listens for her to unlock her door   after he has heard her stop typing & promptly hurries out into the hall, to dump his garbage or to check his mail.

He worries her more than the policemen. Who will eventually go away, after they find   or don't find   whomever they're looking for. The way the place is built, the retired highschool teacher probably knows her daily moves more intimately than she does. Just as she can't help knowing every mouse-&-gurgle detail of the lovemaking couple upstairs.

She wonders if the retired highschool teacher will be able to distinguish between a radio voice & the live voice of the half-naked punk-object up her flue, who may want to say something after he slides back down.

When she'll present him with a plan of how to escape to get rid of him.

—She may never get rid of him. He may be too numb to leave, & she may not have the guts to lead him by the hand out of the watched building, past the police car at the curb. Undetected even by the retired highschool teacher.

He will spend the night, & the next day, & the night after that. A week. A month. A year. Threatening to call the police & tell them that she pulled him inside every time she tries to push him out. She's stuck with him for life. Beyond her own duration, into all eternity.—

She continues to lean against her open door, not wishing to shut it in the retired highschool teacher's brightened face. He is visibly expecting to be invited into her apartment. Where he has never been. She isn't working now: he heard her stop typing half an hour ago.

Fortunately for her, the policemen are shooing all tenants back behind their respective doors. She closes hers   smiling bright regret at the retiring highschool teacher who turns mechanically & heads back down the stairs.

She walks to her livingroom window & takes up a watching position.

There's much commotion out in the hall & on the stairs. Topped by the incessant high-pitched whine from the absent couple's apartment. It is now whining down the stairs. & the absent couple's apartment door slams shut.

*   *   *

After a while she sees four policemen emerge from the main entrance, carrying a strung-out body in a silver jumpsuit. One side of which is soaked in blood.

She can see the carrying policemen being careful not to let the body bleed onto their uniforms; policemen pay their own cleaning bills.

After another while she disbelievingly recognizes the face of the strung-out silver body as that of the overhead husband. Who normally is home by now. At least that's what she'd always assumed. Assuming that what she normally heard at about this hour were the footsteps of the homecoming husband   & not somebody else's   soon to be followed by the homecoming footsteps of the mouse wife.

Whom she sees rounding the corner of their street.

& breaking into a run at the sight of the police cars in front of their main entrance. & of the ambulance, into which attendants & careful policemen are hoisting the husband's strung-out silver body.

With a bloody flesh-stripped bone hanging off what used to be a shoulder.

Shot off by the half-naked   half-successful   murderer up her flue: she thinks with a shudder.

& starts, & almost cries out, because he's sneezing directly behind her, craning an imprudent neck to see the mouse wife being helped into the ambulance by a policeman.   —With an expeditive pat on the mouse wife's up-ending bottom.

She motions for him to step back from the window   — Does he want the police to spot him?—   Again he obeys, his black pin-prick eyes again searching her face for the reason why she did what she did.

A reason that fully evaporated at the sight of the husband's shot-up shoulder. She pulls down the window shade & turns to face him. He's soot-streaked & shaking, asking: WHY? through chattering teeth.

Because she doesn't like to see half-naked bodies running

from uniforms with axes: she says.   —Truthfully. In keeping
with her philosophy.—   That, & the ice cold drizzle.

Huh? You like naked bodies?

There is a pointed primness to his mouth. Which becomes
primmer as he grins, baring wide-spaced pointed teeth.

She shrugs. She doesn't tell him that she'd have done the
same for a wet cat. She doesn't wish to offend the species of
someone who may be used to settling arguments by shooting.
Even if he looks too numb to do anything. & has no gun. But
there are knives in her kitchen. A hammer. A small handsaw.
All the necessary props for a horrorfilm scenario.

Which she quickly suppresses, lest she imprint the
image on his   apparently vacant & therefore all the more
receptive   mind.

Forcing herself to think instead that she'll get out of this
situation as inadvertently & philosophically as she got into it.
She's safer letting him think that she is after his   slightly
knock-kneed   body.

A thought she visibly reinforces in his mind when she
suggests that he take a hot bath.

There's a different look in his eyes   no longer questioning; almost smug   as he obediently follows her into the bathroom: Now he knows why she pulled him inside.

She refrains from suggesting further that he wash the
orange out of his hair   or cut if off, if it doesn't wash out
to make himself less conspicuous for his exit from the building.
He is obviously   unjustifiably   vain about his appearance,
& might turn actively hostile if he hears her practical suggestion
as disapproval. The stereotype establishment reaction to his
stereotype anti-establishment looks. Which might shake his
newly found trust in her concupiscence.

—Perhaps he will consent to pulling her black stocking
cap down over his ears, when she presents him with her plan for
getting him past the police car at the curb.—

If the police car is still sitting at the curb. She doesn't
dare check, in case they see her lift the window shade which they

may have seen her pull down. On orange bristles craning behind her, watching the mouse wife being patted on her butt.

He may also take offense if she shows herself too eager to be rid of him.

He has started running the water, & she turns the radio on. For the benefit of the retired highschool teacher downstairs. Who probably is still watching the street from his livingroom window.

For whose benefit she also refrains from returning to her typewriter while the bathwater is running. To "The Infections of the Inner Ear," for which her editor will send a messenger at 9:00 a.m. tomorrow. She still has seventeen pages to go.

Which she carries to the livingroom table, & tries to translate soundlessly, in long hand   —with wet palms: her pencil is smudging all over the manuscript—   while she waits for the bather to come out of the bathroom.

Wearing her striped terrycloth robe & slippers.

He sits down across from her in the corner of the couch, letting her robe fall open to show a   gaping   leopard. He's AC-DC: he tells her: He can play any role she wants him to play.

He doesn't believe that her jeans & black turtleneck sweater which she takes off & trades him for her robe aren't implements of her own sexual fantasy: disguising him as herself, as a turn-on.

That she means for him to leave, in that disguise.

With an additional black stocking cap pulled over his telltale hair.

—Carrying a fat manila envelope, filled with copies of a previous translation, & bearing the name & address of a publisher. To show to the two policemen at the curb   if they're still sitting in their car at the curb, questioning anyone leaving   or entering   the building.

To tell the two policemen   if they're still there, & ask   that he's a messenger, sent to pick up a manuscript in apartment 2W.

Which is something that happens routinely, as the probably still watching retired highschool teacher in 1W will readily confirm. If necessary.

Especially if he has heard her buzz the messenger in.

Which she will do right now: he has 1 to 3 minutes to get out.

He doesn't believe that she means it. & is baring his wide-spaced pointed teeth in a knowing grin: he's getting the picture.

As long as she doesn't climax turning the messenger in: he grins.

Although: He's clean. They got nothing on him. They can't nail him for not sticking around when that stupid mother started playing with his rifle.

She finds it hard to believe that the upstairs husband aimed at his own shoulder. But she says nothing. Who was trying to shoot whom is none of her business. Her business is "The Infections of the Inner Ear." Which she must finish if it takes all night.

She does mean it: she says earnestly: She's got work to do.

She hopes he won't insist, but if that's the only way to get rid of him, she'll go through with it. She'll close her eyes, & concentrate on Simone Weil, hoping that he has neither herpes, nor amoebas, nor any other fashionable disease currently preying on the promiscuous.

Although: How does she know that he's promiscuous? She's committing the very sin of majority judgment she wanted to counter-balance by throwing her impetuous featherweight onto the lighter scale.

But: He thought she was hurting. He doesn't see no man around.

She shrugs. She got carried away: she says.   —Truthfully again, though not in the sense she allows him to hear. She must finish all these pages by 9:00 a.m. tomorrow: she says, tapping the pages with a sweaty hand.

Okay. Okay.

He isn't as offended as she'd expected him to be. In *her* vanity. He isn't that interested; he's numb.

But not numb enough to obey her this time. He isn't going anywhere for real, dressed like this. In her clothes. When he's got his own stuff lying upstairs. His 400$ leather jacket from Spain. His 200$ boots. His 180$ black leather pants. He's going back upstairs & get them.

Maybe he'll come back down with some cocaine. If they didn't take it. If that mother didn't flush it down the toilet 16,000$ worth   after shooting himself in the shoulder.

That mother would have done better to sweep the borax up from along outside their door when the sirens started coming. The police may be stupid, but not stupid enough to think that that borax along outside their door was put there to keep out the roaches. They know what it means: That it means that a new supply has come in.

Has she ever tried cocaine sex? Nice. Real smooth.

She escorts him to her bedroom window & lets him out. Relocking it after him. Watching his feet disappear on the rain-polished iron. Hoping that she won't see them coming back down, in case the police locked the upstairs window.

She kneels beside her typewriter, muttering a prayer of relief when she hears his footsteps overhead. He has put on his 200$ boots, & is pacing.

But he isn't leaving. & may, of course, be preparing to come back down. With or without cocaine. Tomorrow she'll have gates put on the bedroom window.

She forces herself to start typing. After a while she hears the pacing stop. Perhaps he has sacked out on the absent couple's bed.

She has translated eleven of the seventeen pages when she hears the mouse wife walk into the upstairs foyer. Around 1:00 a.m. She hears his footsteps wake up & go to meet hers. Together they walk into the bedroom.

She hears a long muffled conversation   followed by silence   followed by long gusts of muffled laughter. Which eventually culminates in the familiar squeak.

Which continues on & off, off & on, paragraphing her translation. It's on   on on on: sustained by cocaine? she wonders   when she types her name after the last word: ear, at 3:38 a.m.

She's awakened by her bell at exactly 9:00 a.m. & staggers to open her door. To face an orange-bristled, black-leathered messenger. Who grins knowingly as he asks for the manila envelope.

The Cyclotaur

HE COMES WALKING TOWARD HER from the far end of their street   across the sun-streaked avenue   with that peculiar aquatic shuffle of his: as though his feet were fins, gracefully slicing paved gray water. His motorcycle helmet sits in the crook of one arm. The other arm stretches wide in anticipation of their hug.

She checks his eyes. They're warm & shiny. She opens her arms. He's the most loving man she knows. They have more in common than the plausible couples. (They meditate together.) They're implausible only in the street.

"He must be stupid," two young Blacks tell each other, shaking their earrings as they pass him hugging her.

He hasn't heard them. Or if he has, he isn't taking it for himself. They don't mean him: they're not into conventional street behavior. They're his brothers, dressed as he is in the uniform of the non-conforming. They've seen his earring.

A gold serpent biting its tail: the symbol of unending life. It was his idea for wedding bands; a surprise present for her on the third anniversary of their living together.

She had hers remade into a regular ring, which she wears on her left little finger. She didn't want to have a pin stuck through one of her balance centers: she says.

32

He says: She was scared of the pain. Her fear of a pin prick is greater than her commitment to their relationship.

To which he is more committed than she is: he tells her: Or else she'd let him work with her. On the new animal footage from Nairobi, instead of hiring the new assistant she just hired.

After firing the old one.

Who was probably sick of kowtowing to her bossiness. Wasn't that why she fired him? Wasn't it? Wasn't it?

She walks to the window, away from his voice. She doesn't dare remind him of what he knows better than she does: That staring fixedly at a source of light   especially a tiny source of light, like a movieola screen   for hours every day would be a direct invitation to the cyclotaur.

Whose existence he denies.

Although he has, on occasion, taken pride in his kinship with certain great names of the past: Cesar   Alexander Dostoievski. Whose otherness he shares.

The centaurs.

The Minotaur. His patron saint, whose beastly half had   incidentally   been strictly vegetarian. While the human part fed on yearly supplies of adolescent Athenians.

Which was less barbaric than dehorning generations of adolescent cattle, before permitting them to grow up into beef. He believes in the equality of all that lives. They both do.

It was certainly a lot less hypocritical than the daily sacrifices she exacts from him. As her ritualistic lackey. Her escort service. Her camera-carrying mule.

He knows what she thinks of him: he hisses through clenched teeth: She thinks that he can do nothing. Except maybe sing to her. & sit at her feet. She always makes him feel unworthy.

She won't even give him the benefit of a try, with the Nairobi footage. When she knows that he knows animals. Prob-

ably better than her new assistant. Who's probably running her
an ego bath.

She knows he spent his boarding school boyhood watching cats & dogs & horses & cows. He knows exactly when
they're about to lift a hoof, or pick up their ears. He could cut
animal footage better than anybody.

Better than she could, probably. Which is probably why
she won't risk giving him the chance. In case he turns out to be
better than she is. Which is fine with him. He understands. He
won't be a threat to her ego mirage. He's leaving.

But he continues to sit: in her bathrobe, sex exposed
above crossed knees. Coarse, suddenly. All grace drained from
body & face.

His eyes are dull; opaque. His voice is a leaden drone as
he lists more & more instances of her bossiness; her selfish disregard & lack of understanding.

Humiliations inflicted on him by their friends.

Who are *her* friends, not his.

Their relationship is much harder on him, socially, than
it is on her. She may get slanting smiles or a raised eyebrow,
because people think she's a hot old bitch.   —Which isn't even
true. Not anymore. When just the opposite is true.—   But
nobody would dream of suggesting that she might be taking
advantage of him. Everybody always thinks that he's taking advantage of her.

When just the opposite is true. He's always being treated
like an appendage, at the screenings she drags him to.   —To
which she can go by herself, from now on. He's leaving.—
He doesn't enjoy playing second fiddle wherever they go.

He's worse off than the female wives, who are at least
applauded for playing their second fiddles. But gigolos don't get
applause. Or bodyguards. Which is always how he is made to
feel. By her friends, who won't even bother introducing him.

Not to mention that adoptive father of hers, who has
probably been fantasizing about getting into her pants ever since
she turned pubescent.

Which certainly wasn't yesterday.

He is trapped in one of his rages. Which seem to recur in cycles, like menstruation. It's like a bleeding of his soul that keeps filling up with pain. There's nothing she can do but wait it out.

She comes back from the window & sits down across from him.

"Let me finish!" His teeth are clenched. As are his fingers. The loving man who brought coffee to her bed that morning has disappeared behind a wall of hate.

She isn't saying anything. She sits waiting, the round marble table between them. It is early afternoon on a sunny Saturday. They had taken their time having coffee in bed. & cigarettes. Cuddling with her   their   cats. Happily: she'd thought. Leaning into each other, legs intertwined, exchanging the groping esoteric speculations they both like so much. She'd thought he'd hardly noticed   or minded   when she got up to take a bath before their speculations started groping for sex.

He had taken a bath after her. With more coffee, & more cigarettes.   —Which were the ritualistic forerunners of the cyclotaur, sometimes. If she were less self-indulgent, she'd give up smoking.

He'd been lying back in the tub, listening to a tape he'd made the night before, of himself singing & playing the guitar while stoned. He hasn't liked what he heard. He won't get stoned again. He's leaving.

She doesn't know what she dreads more: the dull droning of hatred or the takeover by the cyclotaur.

Under the table his toes curl & uncurl. But his mind is hanging onto the mechanized voice. Finally he packs a bag & leaves. In a dead white silence. Dark distrusting animal eyes darting reproaches at her from a dead white face.

She locks the door behind him & returns to sit in her chair. Feeling homeless, in her apartment. & old.

But also released. To her, each departure feels final.

She's always surprised   —a gasp of gladness mixed with dread—   when he comes back.

An hour   a week   five months   later. She checks his eyes: they're warm & shiny. They hug. They go to sleep holding hands.

Why does she always let that boy come back? asks her adoptive father. Who never knew her to be a masochist before. Nor particularly self-sacrificing.

That boy isn't a boy. He's a man. & more mature than some older men she knows.

Her adoptive father frowns.

Did her adoptive father think of himself as a boy when *he* was 28?

No. Because, at 28, her adoptive father was supporting not only a wife, but also his wife's two-year-old daughter. Her "man" isn't normal.

Probably not. What normal   better-than-normal-looking   28-year-old would love a woman twice his age. Which he does. He does love her.

Which mocks the pragmatic laws of nature. & must therefore come to a bad end. Her adoptive father is concerned. He'd hate to see her come to harm.

He has never hurt her.

Not yet.

She shrugs.   —She has never told anyone what an experience it can be, watching a lover turn into a motorcycle.

Which may be her punishment   she sometimes thinks   for having evaded a responsibility once, many years ago, during a bus trip to Florida. When she'd gone to visit her adoptive father & her adoptive father's then-current girlfriend: Grace, was it? Or Lucille?

She had been sitting by a window on the bus, when she'd felt stared at   checked out   by an old couple towing a teenage girl. Soon after, the male half of the couple had climbed on & installed the girl in the seat next to hers. Asking her: PLEASE! to make sure his teenage granddaughter didn't go to sleep. Because his teenage granddaughter had psycho-motor problems, which manifested mainly in sleep.

She had said neither yes nor no to the grandfather. Feeling presumed upon, because of potential motherliness in her looks, her   already then   responsible age.

She'd stared without expression into the smiling eyes of the old couple who had stood, reunited on the platform, making reassuring gestures to their granddaughter, & responsibility-engaging gestures to her, through the bus window. But as soon as the bus got under way, she had climbed over the girl's outstretched legs, & found another seat way in the back.

She's responsible if she gets hurt: she says. Annoying her adoptive father.

Whom she reminds of an annoying Italian neighbor, who used to go around telling people that they'd be not only responsible, but guilty, if they got themselves murdered: for having kept the appointment.

—An appointment that could last for all eternity, in early-Renaissance Provence. Whose laws buried caught murderers with their victims, in a single coffin, the live murderers often tied to their dead victims.—

The annoying neighbor had been a fairly well-known Italian painter of wide-eyed, Greek-nosed women stringing cats' cradles with fishing nets.

He used to keep a caged canary on his window sill, & a fat white cat that used to sit on top of the canary cage. Forever reaching a six-toed paw through the wires, while the canary pecked at the trailing white tail. Finally, one day, their neighbor had found his cat sitting on top of the empty cage, disconsolately looking at a heap of yellow feathers.

The neighbor had not buried his cat with the canary feathers. In fact, he had not punished his cat at all. Taking full blame for setting up the canary's appointment.

Which may have been his intention: prodding life to inspire art. Because shortly thereafter he had painted a very large painting of a white Greek-nosed woman with wide slanted eyes, sitting atop an oversize bird cage, amidst a sea of yellow feathers. Which he had called: *The Disconsolate Redeemer of Caged Flight.*

Her still annoyed adoptive father shakes his head: He hates to see his mature, level-headed daughter so hung up.

She shrugs.

Rather than explain that this relationship has less & less to do with sex. At least on her side. They don't make love very often. If at all.

Which he lists as another reason for leaving, when the next cycle comes around.

He has forgotten that they used to make love as often as he'd let her, before the first couple of times he left. After they first started living together. Please: he'd say: I'm tired. Rolling out of reach to the far side of the bed.

Which has become her position: Out of reach of his reaching arms.

It's not that he does not attract her anymore: she tells him, evading his desire.

Their love has outgrown the need for routine conjugal climaxes: she tells him: the "twice a week" recommended by the rebelliously conjugal Martin Luther.

Her love for him is like a constant embrace: she tells him. Rolling out of reach.

She has been asking herself if she has once again come to the end of a desire span. Based on past experience: 3 years . . . 1½ . . . 1 year? Before friendship takes over. Before the all-too familiar body next to hers begins to feel like family. Like an adopted father. & she feels like wrapping herself in saran wrap before bedding down, to protect her skin from the incestuous touch.

Perhaps she suffers from skin fatigue. Which turns to repulsion when pushed.

But he does not repulse her. Not at all. She loves to feel the touch of his skin against hers. To lie in his arms, quietly, & look at him.   —"Drop": he says, stretching one arm under her neck. He's the tenderest man she knows. & aesthetic to look at. She loves his face, especially from the side. The curve of his nose has such delicate strength.

She has tried asking other women about the length of their desire spans. Do they still feel like making love to the bodies of the men they've been living with for 3 . . . 7 . . . 20 years?

Of course they do: they tell her. With a quizzical look. A frown of misgiving. It gets better and better: they tell her.

Or else they complain about their man's loss of interest. Never mentioning/always denying their own.

Perhaps it's her age: One day the sex urge simply drops away. With a sigh of relief. Now she can hire her assistants for their professional   rather than their physical   qualifications. It's a great freedom.

Which may not be her conscious spiritual achievement so much as biology. In which case she can't expect his body to be ready for cuddling continence, whether they meditate together or not.

She had hoped that meditation might drive out the cyclotaur. Following the recipe of medieval exorcism, that pitted the positive energy of God against a visiting demon.

& perhaps he had hoped the same. But it hadn't worked. On the contrary: Twice, toward the end of sitting side by side, cross-legged in front of a candle for twenty minutes, fixing their eyes on the bridge of their noses, the cyclotaur has appeared in full force.

To her surprise he almost talks about it in front of their friend Malcolm, during a dinner.

Malcolm has come without his brother Bertram, & is telling them why Bertram didn't join them: Bertram had an out-of-body experience during his evening meditation, & upon returning found his body occupied by another entity. He had to fight long & hard to gain reentry. He felt too exhausted to go out.

"The atmosphere is full of disgruntled spirits looking for a body": Malcolm says: "If you leave yourself open . . . unaware . . ."

He nods. "Twice, after meditating . . .": he begins. But he checks himself. The word unaware annoys him. Maybe Bertram is unaware, but not he.

Suddenly he has forgotten who Bertram is. Bertram? He asks. What Bertram? Isn't Bertram a cat?

He makes a cult of cats. & quotes a famous painter whose name he can't remember. Who said that: in case of a fire, if he had to choose between saving a Rembrandt or a cat he'd save the cat.

So would he: he says.

In perpetual atonement for the cat he once hanged, when he was a 12-year-old boy in a boarding school. When he was the only boy in the boarding school who couldn't go home for the Christmas holidays. Which he was made to spend with the school superintendent & his family because his parents were self-involved in divorcing each other & needed all their psychic energy for getting even.

On Christmas morning he picked up the school superintendent's cat & hanged it from their Christmas tree.

She let me tie my belt around her neck: he says: She trusted me.

His memory comes & goes, remote-controlled by unknown outside forces. Living with him is reference-less. Each day starts from zero.   —The only way Kafka could cope with his unbearable life.—   Each morning she checks his eyes, &

again in the evening, when he comes home from work, to see
what kind of time they'll be spending together.

But he has left once again. She no longer needs to sit in
the cyclotaur's waiting room. She's independently lonely.

Her own age once again: a gray-haired cutter of films,
with a studio just off Times Square.

Outside the narrow studio window, a pair of gigantic
black-booted legs tirelessly walk along a gray wall. Advertising
something. Johnny Walker probably. The window is too low for
her to see the total man. Or his message. She sees only the
incessant up-&-down movement of the enormous legs. Which
look clumsy, out of context. Compulsive. They make her think
of the cyclotaur.

She has asked her new Czech   Italian-toothed   assistant to keep the shade pulled down even when they're not working at the movieola.

It's her film-archives memory that makes her think of the
new assistant as: Italian-toothed. Although she has traveled in
Italy enough to know that average Italian teeth   average Euro-
pean teeth in general   are less limelighted than teeth in America. Besides, the new assistant is Czech. But every time she looks
at him, her memory unwinds reel upon reel of Latin lovers,
baring remarkable teeth.

He's not her type.

The teeth of the cyclotaur are differently remarkable:
They're clenched.

She hopes she wouldn't have hired the new Italian-
toothed Czech assistant if he *were* her type. Not at this stage in
her life. Especially not if he were her type, & did not possess the
new assistant's surprising eye for cutting.

Which may be congenital. The Czech national affinity
with visual effect in film & theatre. Italians seem to have such
an affinity with stone. & Portuguese with flower arrangements.
& Anglo-Saxons with suicide.

The new assistant works hard for her approval. He smiles a great deal because he has good teeth & speaks bad English. This is his first job in America. In New York City. It does not occur to him that there might be a private side to her, outside the cutting room. He doesn't think of gray-haired women as women. He is a normal 28-year-old. Instead he thinks of making a film of his own, like other normal   less gifted   assistants before him.

It's an ambition she has never shared. Not once during the almost thirty years that she has worked with film. Which may be why filmmakers like to work with her: She thoroughly knows her craft & lets them be   or feel   creative.
        Although, for quite some time now she has been thinking of shooting the cyclotaur.
        Which is not an ambition, but rather an attempt at self-justification. She would like to make a documentary of what happens when it happens. To show to him. Afterward, when it's over. When he has no recollection of anything. & denies that anything did happen.
        Which seems to happen only when they're alone.
        She is making it up: he says: to justify not making love anymore.
        Shaking her reality. Not because she distrusts her senses. & isn't sure of what she has witnessed   15, maybe 20 times by now; 15 to 20 variants of the same dark ritual   but because of the insidious truth that sometimes lurks behind his wildest accusations. Perhaps she avoids making love because her body has grown afraid: seeing itself pinned under a primal motorcycle.

I am not afraid of cyclotaurs: she overhears a producer's wife say to him after a screening. During the traditional party that follows a screening.
        He must have been drinking, to mention the cyclotaur to the fearless producer's-wife. After complaining about his sex-exempt second-fiddle existence. He, too, feels like a wife at these screenings: he says: Like an unappreciated backdrop.

He leaves with the fearless producer's-wife. Who tosses her a challenging look. & she asks her assistant to put her in a cab.

If he hadn't left, they'd be walking the twenty-four blocks to the apartment. It's a brilliant night. The kind of perfect weather historically recorded for the starting days of wars, & great depressions.

She's sure this departure is the last: He never had anyone to help him leave before.

But helping a fearless wife get even with her indifferent producer husband   —who smiles fatherly encouragement every time they run into each other, on their respective ways into or out of the producer's apartment building—   offends his sense of loyalty.

He comes back, steeped in guilt. He'd had too much to drink, at that stupid screening party. After watching almost two hours of mostly sex. If they made love more often . . .

What has happened to us? he asks: Do I repulse you?

She assures him that he doesn't. & kisses him, to prove to him that he doesn't.

There is that strange smell again   like lead   which seems to come from his nostrils, announcing the approach of the cyclotaur, a couple of hours, sometimes a whole day before it happens.

She would like to tell him about the smell. To warn him. But he's on his way out. She doesn't want to make him feel insecure in the street. At his job. In case it started happening when they're not alone.

For which she wishes, sometimes. Despising herself. Why couldn't he have turned into a motorcycle & run over the fearless producer's-wife?

She also wonders if it's maybe her presence that has been bringing it on. Perhaps he's allergic to her. Since it never happened before they started living together.

had been living together for a little over a year the
appened. In his sleep   —when it was supposed to
___ to the old couple's granddaughter, whom she had
failed to keep awake on the bus to Florida.

That first time he had not awakened until it was over.
Shaking his head at her description of what had happened. Asking: If she hadn't maybe had a bad dream.

But believing her, finally. He still trusted her then.

She isn't sure when he started accusing her of making it
up. Despite bruises, now. A deep cigarette burn on his inner
thigh. It's happening more & more often.

Perhaps he's allergic to her age.

They're lying side by side in the big double bed. The
white cat is curled up on his feet. The black cat is snoring on her
pillow beside her face.

She wakes up. He is speaking in his sleep. First we got
to get the old woman's leg out of the way: he says, still articulate.
Vigorously kicking her nearest leg.

He has kicked off the covers. His toes are clenched. The
cyclotaur is revving his motor.

The white cat flies up the flue above the fireplace. The
black cat stays to watch:

The slow sideways turn of the head, as though pulled into
a different dimension by unseen clamps. Guttural sounds, like a
deaf-mute screaming.

His hands clutch at the lamp for support. It breaks in his
grip. The lampshade rolls under the bed.

His body rolls after it. Missing the pillow   her robe
she throws down to cushion his crash.

He is lying on his back, with furiously revving feet &
arms. The forehead hitting upward against the iron frame of the
bed. His chest is bleeding below the left nipple, where he grinds
the broken porcelain stump of the lamp into his flesh.

* * *

When it's completely over, the white cat reappears, sooty, ghost-like, cautiously sniffing his toes.

Every return is different. Sometimes there is only exhaustion. Mildness; even a brief muffled song. At others, it seems to take forever for his mind to return behind his eyes, while the raging continues, threatening to bash her face in with the camera she brought home from the studio.

Which she'd been keeping under the bed. In a box, to keep the cats from doing their claws on it. She didn't think he knew it was there.

So far she hasn't been able to use it. She's afraid to turn up the light & shine it on him like a maddening third degree. Besides, she's always throwing pillows. Moving table edges & objects   herself   out of his way.

Which should also be in the documentary she wants to make. To show to him & prove that she hasn't been making up anything.

A documentary of the cyclotaur would also serve to prove his innocence in court, in case she weren't able to dodge his onslaught, one day. Or night.

In which case no judge of any era or area would condemn him to being buried with her. In the same coffin. His live youthful body bound to her dead old one. Unable to leave until total disintegration took over.

But he has left once again. This time surely his departure is final. Her adoptive father need no longer be concerned about her safety. She is once again independently lonely.

Her own age once again: a gray-haired cutter of film, with a studio window looking at the back of Times Square.

She pulls up the shade which her new Italian-toothed Czech assistant had quickly pulled down at her entry, & stands watching a screening of the cyclotaur.

He comes walking toward her from the far corner of the

Rites of Non-Requital

HANG-UPS ARE TRADITIONALLY TOLD from the unrequited end. Because the victim always writes. At first to the unrequiting object. & when the object fails to respond, the victim addresses the world. The victim's lament becomes objectified by echo. Whose harrowed calls indict the object:

Objects aren't moving.

Objects are cold. Jagged icicles of selfishness that resist the hottest tears.

Whereas the lamenting victim exudes pure   wasted love. Which those who hear the echo would not have let go to waste.

Unless the object is actively cruel. In that case, listeners to the echo might find their attention shifting to technical details. Which might impress them as being more creative than the victim's self-created pain. In that case, they might even absolve the object, compelled by admiration for the object's technique.

But cruelty would be a form of requital. Which would require a different ritual.

The object of the present hang-up is benign. At least at the outset.

So are tumors: sighs the echo. Anticipating the lament of the as-yet-not-unrequited party:

46

Male. A tall, slightly stooped soil analyst with skinny hair who works at the United Nations.

His fantasy has as yet not crystallized into obsession. It is just beginning to fasten on the   as yet benign   object:

Female. Past the age of reproduction, &   she hopes past the age of acting on impulses of the flesh.

She has been hung up herself a number of times. Though usually not without requital. On the most unlikely objects: like an astonished delivery boy when she was in her forties.

Yet, she'd look for companionship in these unlikely objects. Kneeling   with condescension   to luminous skin or butterfly eyelashes, for spans of requited ecstasy that lasted as long as she could stay on her knees. Sometimes as long as one year, a year & a half. Until the unlikely objects' unlikely minds or demands began overshadowing their bodies. When she'd resume a standing position; driving them away.

Unfortunately for her   in the society that feeds her she has rarely been attracted to a contemporary body.

Whose aesthetic appeal has mostly been replaced by the body's position in the world. On the basis of which the mostly no longer aesthetic body feels qualified to express opinions about   her   art. Even if the body's worldly position is rooted in the stockmarket. Or in dentistry. Which the body considers serious work, which required serious   & expensive   preparation. Unlike art, especially her so-called abstract art, in which any body can dabble. To which she has recently begun to reply that: She has been thinking of maybe taking up banking, or orthodontia, as a hobby.

As a result she has lately been living alone.

Which worries her occasionally. She has watched other artists live alone. Not all necessarily female, or beyond the age of reproduction. She has watched them grow scaly, from lack of contact with another's skin. Rigid & self-convoluting. She doesn't want prolonged solitude to show up as sterility in her work.

*   *   *

She is a painter/collagiste whose work is known to museums, & critics, & other painters. & to a limited circle of fans. But few galleries like to show her. She's what they call: a painter's painter. She doesn't sell well enough for them to make a profit. Or for herself to live on.

That's why she teaches the evening classes the soil analyst is taking. Twice a week, on Wednesdays & Fridays.

To improve his color sense.   —He may be slightly color-blind: he tells the class. The soon-to-be-objectified teacher. He has always enjoyed sketching the landscapes of field trips: he says: & might want to try his hand at illustrations of travel books when he retires.

—Unless their teacher thinks that he's talented enough to become an avant-garde painter like herself . . .

Which she discourages. Not unless he's independently wealthy: she says. With a cordially indifferent smile.

At the beginning of a semester she routinely cautions her students not to count on their art to support them. But she also encourages them, when they show promise.   —Like the Indian student, from Idaho. Who shows more than promise, actually. Who is truly talented. He also has the type of body that might have prompted an impulse of her flesh, in her still active past.—

Occasionally she'll also encourage a student who shows no promise at all. When the student is elderly. Like the soil analyst, for whom art may be therapy.

She treats everyone with the same cordial indifference.

Which the objectifying soil analyst interprets as personalized cordiality, subtly intended for him alone.

He is the oldest student in her class. Though possibly a year or two younger than she is. Still: a contemporary body. She notices nothing   beyond his skinny hair, & a reddish-glazed complexion attributable to broken capillaries rather than UN field trips   when he assures her that: He can afford to become an avant-garde painter. He will be more than secure when he retires from the UN. At this point in his life he has only himself to take care of.

He is beaming. Objectifying her. Interpreting her cordially indifferent remark as a subtle inquiry into the financial situation of a man who has caught her interest. He is after all her only contemporary in the room. Her ally on the experience side of the generation gap.

He starts bringing offerings to class: baskets of flowers & exotic fruit. A bonsai tree. Lacquered Japanese boxes. Which he asks her to set up as models for the class to draw. Or to paint.

—In keeping with the ritual, the unrequited party totally disregards the object's   or anyone else's   plans.—

Which the class is free to pursue: she tells him. Just as he is free to work with whatever he brings in. Preferably in color though, if he wishes to improve his color sense.

He hasn't heard her. He has started drawing. With reddish-glazed zeal. His fantasy is supplanting the reality of her cordial indifference: she doesn't want the class to profane his offerings. Chosen with visualizations of her hands touching his offerings as she sets them up.

Which she doesn't.

After class he takes them to her, urging her to take them home.

She accepts his baskets, but then profanely stands by the door, inviting the others to help themselves on their way out.

& she flatly refuses to touch either the bonsai fir or his nest of boxes.

Which his spited fantasy tries to explain:

a) as diplomacy. Perhaps school policy frowns on teachers accepting gifts from their students. Or

b)   —& this troubles him—   as a dislike for things Japanese. Which strikes him as an incomprehensible limitation on the part of a professionally sensitive person.

* * *

A person with whom his fantasy has begun to live in the closest intimacy. There simply is no room for differences of taste.

Which his fantasy stubbornly tries to explain away:

He hadn't appreciated dwarfed, lacquered sensibility or raw fish   either, before his travels in Japan. *He* will teach *her,* perhaps starting with Japanese prints.

—He tries not to see the cigarette she lights after class. *He* gave up smoking eight years ago.—

Unless   & this troubles him more deeply   there has been an unpleasant Japanese-connected experience in her past.

He is rightly troubled: Ritualistically the object's past never occurs to the unrequited party. Whose fantasies are strictly forward directed: Happily ever after . . .

But she obviously has a past, at her age. As he has a past. Even though, according to ritual, she came into being the Wednesday evening she entered the classroom.

Perhaps she does not live alone.

& is not widowed   perhaps not even divorced/or single   with no grown daughter or grown son or both, no longer living at home. Contrary to sub-surface assumptions of his forward-directed fantasy. Which had created a sub-surface past for her, unimaginatively modeled after his own.

It is in keeping with the ritual for the unrequited party to turn detective:

He begins to question fellow students. His trouble slyly disguised as concern about her qualifications as a teacher: Shouldn't they know more about this woman who is trying to make them look at things through her eyes. Does anyone know if she has maybe lived in Japan.

They smile broadly, & suggest that he ask her directly. Or else they refer him to what it says about her in the course description: That her work is well-respected & hangs in several museums.

He doesn't tell them that he spent two whole Saturdays in the two museums in which she hangs.   —Fantasizing that he'd run into her there; that she'd come to check on her paintings.—   He had finally found five of them, & had studied them for the longest time. He doesn't know what to make of them. Perhaps his color blindness is worse than he'd thought. Still, it never kept him from appreciating shapes. He couldn't even recognize the shapes in her paintings. It's as though she lived in a totally different world.

Which his fantasy refuses to acknowledge: It's only a misunderstanding. Which will melt away as soon as she realizes how he feels about her.

He calls the registrar's office & asks for her address & phone number. Which: he is told: the registrar's office does not give out. Instead he is given the phone number of an art gallery.

He calls the art gallery. & gets an answering service. He hangs up. He calls again. He keeps calling until he gets a flat male voice that informs him that it is against gallery policy to give out the phone numbers of artists. & when he lies, & says that he's an art buyer   for Japan   who's interested in her work, the flat male voice gives him precise directions to the gallery. & presses him into making an appointment.

On the way to the gallery his fantasy buys her most expensive painting, & takes it to class for her to inscribe to him. She is so pleased with his choice, & so impressed with what he says about it, that she asks him to her house to show him what she has been working on lately. Something totally different from her former style. Her outlook has completely changed since they met, on that fateful Wednesday evening when he walked into her class.

Into her life. She does live alone. Etc.

But the paintings which the flat-voiced gallery owner places before him   & later, in response to his lack of response holds up against an empty stretch of gallery wall, are again unrecognizable shapes, in colors too muted for him to differentiate.   & far more expensive than the most expensive one his fantasy had purchased on his way over.

He ends up buying two Japanese prints. Which he plans to send to her   anonymously   as soon as her finds out her address. Or else he will come to class early one evening & put them on her desk.

Meanwhile he brings his collection of rock roses to class. Correctly assuming that neither She   —the word is acquiring a capital S as his fantasies travel further & further from reality; soon all three letters will be capitalized—   nor most of his fellow students have ever seen a rock rose.

—Except the Indian student from Idaho. Who immediately sketches one, & holds it up for the class to see.

Earning her praise.

She has been praising the Indian student's work consistently since their first evening of class. It does not occur to the object-focused soil analyst that She might accept from the Indian student what She keeps rejecting from him. Even though she hopes to be beyond the age of acting on impulses of the flesh. He counts on the geological charm of his rock roses to make Her want to take at least one of them home with Her, with Her fantasized Hands.

After he finishes his drawing. He's still working in pen & ink, despite Her urgings to start using color. To try crayons at least, if he's afraid of oil.

He's not afraid of oil. He's afraid that he may use red instead of green.

SHE is touching his upper arm: She wants him to hold up his finished drawing for the class to see. & to criticize. She wants someone else to praise the soil analyst's meticulous copies of eleven rock roses   as she's sure someone will, on the basis of sheer recognition   before she ventures to say that: The greatest accuracy of detail doesn't necessarily depict the essential quality of a thing as accurately as an abstract rendering of it might.

She wishes he'd used that washed-out pink that made the twisted clay look like petrified petals.

He really needs to start working with color: she says: She will not accept another piece from him in pen & ink.

Instead of saying outright that his rock roses look about as inspired as a passport photograph. That his drawing has deprived them of their soul.

Which she might just as well be saying. He doesn't hear HER. His fantasy is flying, touched off her HER HAND on his arm. For one bold moment it merges with reality: He takes HER HAND, & firmly closes HER FINGERS around two of his rock roses. For YOU: he says.

She likes these stone flowers she's seeing for the first time. & is about to accept at least one of them when laughing starts somewhere in the classroom.

She has been vaguely aware of previous classroom reactions to the soil analyst's attempts to monopolize her attention. To which she hadn't given much thought. He's older than they are, & probably used to ordering a secretary around. He may also have genuine trouble with his eyes.

Which can't be what they're laughing about. Then why are they laughing.

She hands the rock roses back to him, with a twinge of regret. No, thank you: she says, moving on to look at another student's work.

At the Indian student's, from Idaho. Who is smiling up at her, with winking complicity. She doesn't know why. & she doesn't like it.

She still hasn't noticed what all of them noticed during their first evening of class. & have been watching ever since: the soil analyst's unrequited hang-up.

They interpret her cordial indifference as cruelty. Which

amuses them. Two old bodies playing teenage games. They're laughing because one of them stage-whispered that: One of these days the old boy was going to model for the class in his birthday suit, & afterward ask the old girl to take him home.

They've been making bets: She will. / She won't. / When . . .

After class, one of those who bet that she would, lays a persuasive hand on the soil analyst's shoulder & urges him to: Try harder, Man. Do something. Why don't you ask her out.

& the Indian student stops her at the door, smiling. Asking: Why she won't take pity on the poor soil analyst & his rock roses.

Which ends this rite of non-requital. By changing the object's cordial indifference to active irritation. Objects have no initiative. Whereas the no-longer benign, actively irritated art teacher has wheeled around & is asking the startled soil analyst: If he's trying to pick her up.

—In verbal imitation of a woman who has been pinched on an Italian street. & who, instead of walking on, in keeping with the ritual that expects her to be flattered by the prospect of a bruise on her behind, spins around, & pinches back. Shocking the pincher into indignant flight.

Her voice is a brilliant icicle, jabbing at this contemporary body that is responsible for her companionless life. The slightly stooping shoulders. His skinny hair. The reddish glaze of his face, which has turned the washed-out pink of twisted clay.

But he is standing his ground. Mute & stooping, his arms reaching for her as though she had asked him to dance.

She sweeps past him   past an audience of lingering students; the still smiling Indian student still at the door   & out of the room.

If the soil analyst doesn't drop the course, the class will be able to watch yet another ritual: Of requital by attrition.

Xmas Tryst

THE XMAS SPIRIT IS SPREADING across the Western hemisphere. Bundles of cut-down pines   evergreen symbols of cutting down the old consort of the Earth Goddess, & crowning the new one   lie stacked at street corners, ready to be bought & taken home by Christian celebrants. To be re-erected in a prominent place of their family room. & decorated with tinsel   & polished winter apples   & people-shaped gingerbreads   & strings of lights that blink on & off like erratic traffic signals, & are modern-technology symbols of the star that allegedly guided the three magi toward the straw bed of the just-born Christ.

Whose actual   Piscean   birthday: Day 1, Year 1, of the Piscean Age, was diplomatically reset for December 25, to coincide with the pagan celebration of the winter solstice, by early Christians tired of martyrdom.

Goaded by holiday expectations two bodies are hurtling toward each other through a tropical winter evening. Heading for collision in a bar in Waikiki. Where the mood is set for Xmas. But instead of a cut-down re-erected pagan pine the bartender has decorated the massive banyan tree around which the bar was built. Leaving large openings in the ceiling to accommodate the thick upper branches. From which hundreds of small lights are blinking Hawaiian rainbows on the patrons' heads. At the foot of the banyan tree, in full view of anyone entering the bar, the original nuclear family has been set up in people-sized effigy: the benignly astonished husband, the bustling, glowing mother, & the chubby wise child that knows its own father. As a reminder to solitary drinkers   natives & tourists alike   that Xmas is a family holiday.

One of the hurtling bodies is male. From Samoa. As massive & looming as the bar's Xmas tree, but devoid of decorations. Except for a thin gold bracelet around his left wrist. He is wearing jeans & a T-shirt that says: HERE TODAY GONE TO MAUI.

The other hurtling body is female. From Virginia. With the pale skin, & pale hair, & forget-me-not blue eyes of the Southern Belles who offer Southern Comfort & Southern Hospitality on Virginia travel posters. VIRGINIA IS FOR LOVERS.

In her Honolulu hotel   where golden-skinned women with hip-long hair advertise Polynesian Hospitality   she is registered as Caucasian. In the streets she's a Haole; the Hawaiian name for non-Oriental non-natives.

She has dressed up for her Xmas dinner in Hawaii, in a clinging blue silk skirt, a sleeveless blue glitter top, & matching blue glitter pumps, with very high heels. She is in very high spirits. Tomorrow she plans to start working on a tan that will be the envy of the office larvae who work for her in Roanoke.

Where winter came early this year; it was 20 degrees, & there was snow on the ground when she drove to the airport, straight from work at the hospital, where she's an administrator.

She must not forget to bring back a present for the headnurse. Priscilla.

The thought of whom makes her giggle. The headnurse Priscilla started her playing the private game   that has become a small mania   every time she walks down a street.

After a delivery, the headnurse Priscilla likes to tell a new mother   a new father; an aunt; anyone she catches poring over a newborn face for resemblances   that the newborn looks just like its mother's insides.

Any face   the poring aunt's or uncle's face   is noth-

ing but the convex replica of a mother's womb: the headnurse
Priscilla tells them. Which always grosses them out.

& makes her giggle. At the crazy resemblances   with
so-called private body parts   she starts seeing for the cushiony
lips & soft-button nose tips she's passing on Kuhio Avenue.
Where she's walking in search of a pleasant bar, to have a pleasant pre-Xmas dinner drink.

With her widowed mother, a pink-haired older Haole,
who looks an even round from her shoulders to her toes   like
a sturdy column or tree trunk   in a flaming-pink muumuu, with
a purple lei around her neck.

Whom she asks to remind her to buy a present to take
back for the headnurse Priscilla.

Before she asks what her mother thinks of these people's
faces. Don't they look soft. Almost tender. Caressable.

The mother stops & smiles at her daughter. Whom she
tells that she looks pretty in her Xmas outfit.

She takes the daughter's arm to climb three steps to the
door of a bar. Opens it, & peers inside. She gasps up at the
enormous tree with its strings of rainbow lights, then beams
down at the almost people-sized holy family, electronically moving their lips to the words of a carol, & decides that they've found
the right place.

From behind the counter a deeply tanned but non-native
looking woman, despite hip-long hair, wishes them a Merry
Xmas. The woman looks in her late thirties, blonde & tired. She
is wearing a strict black dress with strict white trimming, & a
white flower behind one ear. The mother orders a double Bourbon, the daughter a split of champagne. They've climbed onto
adjacent stools & sit expectantly erect.

Actually there are three bodies hurtling toward each other
on their Xmas collision course. But the third body is not sentient,
at least not by usual sentient standards. The third body is a
Godzilla doll, a huge plastic lizard-dragon-crocodile creature, &
it is traveling in the arms of the Samoan. Over whose massive
left shoulder it is looking, its plastic reptile snout nuzzling its
bearer's neck, with a wide plastic-toothed grin.

Which may reflect the holiday spirit of both plastic beast & sentient Samoan. Who does not smile. Whose unsmiling cushion lips are furled around a cigarette in a pensive pout.

Which he transfers to the neck of one of two opened bottles of Coors   one for him, & one for his plastic friend which appeared on the bar the instant he walked in. Before he heaves himself onto the stool next to the pale-haired, pale-skinned, forget-me-not-eyed Haole woman.

Who turns in a ripple of blue glitter & smiles at the tall unsmiling Samoan beside her.

Who just looks at her over his beer bottle.

Merry Xmas: she smiles.

He looks at her.

I like your friend: she smiles, & playfully slaps the plastic reptile snout.

Which jumps into the air, as the shoulder that was its support jerks around, & a large hand shoots out toward her smiling face, belting her backward across mouth & nose.

She sits stunned. Too stunned to scream, or even to speak.

Not believing that blood is running from her nose; that one upper front tooth has been smashed, with a broken piece embedded in her lower lip.

The barmaid is nowhere in sight. & may not have seen what happened. Which happened so fast   the sound of the slap drowned out by a Xmas carol   no one seems to have noticed anything. Not even the mother, who is drinking peacefully.

The Samoan is standing up. He drapes his Godzilla doll across the stool to free both hands. Which are moving toward her face again. This time balled into fists.

But this time they hit air.

She has ducked. Slid off her stool. Kicked off her high-heeled glitter pumps. & is running out the door.

Startling the mother. Who turns & calls: Marjie? Where are you going?

Why is my daughter running? she asks the large man she sees standing behind the vacant stool beside her.

He glances at her briefly, turns, jams his Godzilla doll under one arm, & runs out.

Where's everybody running? the mother asks in the direction of the barmaid.

Who was there a moment ago, but now is not.

The other drinkers sit engrossed in their glasses.

The pale-haired pale pale pale Haole woman is fleeing along Kuhio Avenue. In the opposite direction she walked with her mother before. On stocking feet. With a bleeding face. Pursued by the Samoan with the Godzilla doll under one arm.

People jump out of the way, then stop & stare after her. Or they stop & stare right at her, & she has to run around them. If somebody tripped him she might make it to the hotel: she thinks.

She has visions of throwing herself inside her room. Locking the door, & feeling safe.

& inspecting the damage to her face.

Even in the lobby she'd be safe: she thinks. If she can make it to their hotel. Kuhio Avenue is lined with hotels. She'd be safe in any lobby: she thinks. Any lobby. Any lobby.

She throws herself toward a lighted area under an awning, & rolls down five marble steps as the Samoan kicks her from behind. Hard, like a football. She flies past potted plants & slams against a facing marble wall. Landing on the marble floor with a thud.

She faints. But he keeps kicking her. Kicking her. Kicking her.

He is yelling now: Don't you ever do that again: he yells: Now maybe you won't do that again . . .   Until the police arrive, & she is pronounced dead.

At the trial the weeping mother said that she was a widow. & that her daughter had been her only daughter. Her only child.

Who had been raised to respect other people & their property, & wouldn't think of making disrespectful gestures toward strange men.

Not even in jest.

& that she would never be able to forgive herself for having dragged her daughter into a bar that catered to gorillas & their Godzillas.

At which point she was interrupted & rebuked.

& the defense lawyer quickly jumped up to say that it may have been this kind of attitude precisely   of Caucasian condescension   that his client may have sensed behind his victim's playful slap to his Godzilla's face.

The deeply tanned barmaid   again dressed in strict black, but without white trimmings or flowers, her hip-long hair twisted into a crown on top of her head   said that the Samoan had come to her bar before. With his Godzilla, for whom he'd always order a second beer, like for a friend.

That he was a moderate drinker   only of beer   whom she'd never seen speak to anybody. & that she'd gone to the inner office to call the police when she'd seen the Haole woman start coming on to him. Because, although Haole herself, she had lived on the islands long enough to know not to do that. A friend of hers   a stand-up comedian by profession   had warned her early on to watch her step around Samoan customers. There were no Samoan jokes: her friend had told her. The only Samoan joke he'd sometimes tell was that there were no Samoan jokes. & even then he made sure there were no Samoans in the audience.

She hadn't even seen the woman slap the Godzilla.

The   now sobbing   mother said that she hadn't seen it either. She'd been looking at that gorgeous tree, & watching the holy family move their lips to the Xmas song.

Only when her daughter ran out   & she'd seen blood on the counter   had she realized that something had happened. Something awful, & she'd started calling for help.

But no one   no one . . .

The defense lawyer affirmed that his client had not meant to kill the Caucasian woman. He had only wanted to teach her a lesson.

Liable to Acts of God

AROUND THE CEMETERY the world is gray. Covered with the thick gray mud that is sullenly sliding down from the volcano to the left of the cemetery plateau. It is filling in the valley that used to be the town. Rising above what used to be the roofs of houses. It is leveling all hierarchies. Obliterating directions.

She can no longer find the spot where her studio used to be. Where she has lived for 27 years, cutting stone portraits of animals. Occasionally of people. Butchers, postmen, dignitaries the mayor's wife in the Colombian town where she came as a visiting artist to teach a sculpture workshop for one fall semester, 27 years ago. & stayed, to stay with her lover.

Who did not stay with her.

On whose grave she is sitting. Her back propped against the broad black stone that bears his name in white lettering: Manuel del Ruiz, the dates that frame the 18 years of his life, & the touched-up, blown-up, weather-proofed photograph of him as a schoolboy, which his mother had had inserted into the center of the stone.

Instead of using the granite sculpture he'd made of himself. In her workshop. Which she sent to his mother, to be placed on his grave instead of a tombstone. But which his mother returned. Wordlessly. Refusing to speak to her, after the death of the only son.

To whom the mother had stopped speaking after the only son moved into the studio, directly up the hill from the mother's house.

The mother used to rent out the studio to visiting artists, & had initially rented it out to her also. Befriending her, although she had never befriended any visiting artist before. She'd always felt that artists couldn't be trusted.

The mother had been glad to sell her the studio, glad that her one artist friend decided to stay. Before the mother became aware of her friend's reason for deciding to stay. & felt betrayed.

Doubly betrayed: by her only artist friend, & by her only son.

Whom she tried to have arrested at the studio. After trying to have her friend driven from the town for bedding down with one of her students. After trying to revoke the sale of the studio.

Her lover's grave lies wedged between an as yet stoneless grave-sized rectangle of weeded earth on the left, reserved for the mother, & the grave of his father on the right, marked by an identical broad black stone, with the father's name & date in identical white lettering. The father's name had also been: Manuel del Ruiz. She caresses it with her eyes. To her, the name is a sound portrait of her lover. & perhaps also of her lover's father, whom she never met. Who had died before she came to the town to teach. Who had perhaps looked like her lover when he'd been her lover's age. Before he began to look like the touched-up, blown-up, weather-proofed photograph of the re-tired banker, which his widow had had inserted into the center of his stone.

She can feel the oval rim of her lover's schoolboy photo-graph through her cotton shirt. Branding her back with the blown-up difference in their age. Making him 13 years old, to her almost 60. Instead of his factual 17–18 to her 32, when they met. & became lovers. & lived together for almost a year, until he died. It chafes her satisfaction with sitting where she's sitting: on top of him.

Where she might not mind dying so much, if that is to be her fate. If she can't keep alive until the arrival of rescue workers.

She has often thought about dying, since her lover's death. About places where dying might be easier; or harder. Her own bed in the studio. A hospital ward. A crashing airplane, filled with the sudden fear smell of passengers.

She has often thought about people, whose company might make dying easier   or harder   since she can no longer think about dying in the company of her lover.

Who died in her absence, on the day she flew to Chicago to open an exhibit of her work.

She has often thought about him, lying   for how long?   on the studio floor. After reportedly falling off the metal ladder on which he'd been standing, chiseling arms into a tall block of granite. Which reportedly fell on him   . . . when he tried to hold onto it, perhaps, after he felt the ladder give under his feet.

Reportedly Manuel del Ruiz died in the arms of his mother. Who'd run to the studio directly up the hill from her house, when her maternal heart heard the voice of her only son cry out to her.

Unless his mother had run to the studio as soon as she heard that her one, one-time artist friend had flown to Chicago. From the postman, perhaps . . .

Perhaps the mother had been standing in the doorway of the studio, berating her only son high up on his ladder, in yet another attempt to retrieve him, when the ladder . . . etc. . . . .

She didn't know that he was dead when she came back from Chicago. He was not at the airport. Or at the studio. Which looked ransacked, with the block of granite lying in the middle of the floor. Next to the bent metal ladder.

She found out about his death from a report in the week-old newspaper in the studio mailbox.

She wonders how the newspaper will report *her* death.
—If there still is a newspaper, in the mud-leveled town.—
If they will disinter the 27-year-old "scandal" of the student-teacher love affair, if she's found dead on her lover's grave.

Where she'd run blindly   without thinking about places where it might be easier or harder to die   when she heard the enormous explosion. & somehow found herself standing outside her dangling studio door, one hand clasped around one horn of her goat.

Pabla, named for Picasso, who'd also had a pet goat. Which one of his wives had one day given away to passing Gypsies. Making a deep cut into their eroding marriage.

She had felt glad, sometimes, that her lover died when he did. Before their life together had time to crumble under the pressure of his silent, actively hostile mother.

She'd seen the mountain boil over. & her goat had started to run. Up the hill. Very fast. She'd run alongside it, holding onto the horn.

You saved us: she says to the goat. Which is now lying across her outstretched legs. Its udder feels soft & cool against her shins. Her right hand is retracing the bony spine, mechanically disentangling terse brown hairs.

Or maybe you just prolonged our dying: she says: Maybe we'll slowly rot, or dry up, & disintegrate, like tired marriages. Like the flowers in the tin cans on the graves all around us.

I'll die when your udder dries up. & you'll die soon after. Of grief. After you've eaten every blade of grass & dead flower & licked every tin can you can find. Maybe you'll last until the gray mud turns hard. Enough for you to run across it, looking for surviving vegetation. But you'll hate to leave my body, so you'll eat that too. & turn into a wild goat, & roam the devastated landscape. Until surviving people spot you, & trap you, & make a roast of you.

Unless the equalizing gray mud has leveled biological hierarchies also. & the surviving people pet you, & share a surviving leaf with you, because they've become vegetarians; or cannibals.

Surviving people have come into the cemetery. She hears panting, & slurring steps. The sighs of exhausted bodies collapsing into positions of rest.

Steps have stopped slurring behind her lover's tombstone. She hears panting directly behind her, & knows without looking around that if she is meant to die in the cemetery, she will die in the company of her lover's mother.

Who casts a tall bony shadow as she limps to stand in front of her. Or rather: in front of the only son's grave. Whose desecration by the presence of the surviving traitor & her surviving goat the mother stands contemplating. With unfocused eyes.

The mother's left foot has lost its shoe. The toes look deep red, like raw meat. The legs are bare, & scratched.

The mother must have run up the hill from her house slightly below the studio. From a slightly greater distance. Perhaps the mother started running slightly later, uphill, against the oncoming downward slide of melted mountain.

What is she to say to this woman who has refused to speak to her for 26^1/2 years. After six months of animated friendship. Instead of being glad that her only son fell in love with the only visiting artist she had deemed worthy of befriending.

Should she comment on the mother's toes & legs. & perhaps offer the tongue of her goat, to lick the injured skin & make it heal faster.

Although the mother does not seem to be aware of the state of her toes & legs.

Nor of anyone sitting on the only son's grave. Onto which the mother may sink at any moment. On top of the unnoticed desecrator & her unnoticed goat. Unless she speaks to the mother. Quickly. Maybe yells to the mother. Hey! Watch out!

Or gives up her place on top of her lover's grave. One of the good places to die.

Which she does. She pats her goat to stand, & stands up with it, her arms around its neck.

Which the mother doesn't notice, in her dazed state. As her scratched-up legs slowly fold beneath her. & she drops into a kneeling position onto the grave of the only son, her unfocused eyes level with his schoolboy photograph.

Unless the mother is fully aware   & is pretending to be unaware   to drive the desecrator from the grave of the only son without having to speak to her.

Although she has begun to speak to the photograph of the only son.

Whom she is telling about the explosion of the mountain. & about the lost house that has been buried under gray mud. That would have been his lost house, if he were still alive, & had come to his senses, & come back to live with his mother. & about the loss of the studio, which has also been buried in the mud. & about the death of his one-time teacher & lover, her one-time artist friend, who ran uphill to the cemetery to die on his grave, together with her goat, but is being forced outside the cemetery walls, & pushed off the plateau into the still sliding gray mud, by indignant townspeople. Who are keeping her goat, with which they're planning to feed themselves until they are rescued by Red Cross helicopters.

Dr. Arnold Beidermeier's Suicide Parlors

[a way out of the ordinary]

IT WAS IN AESTHETIC SELF-DEFENSE that Dr. Arnold Bieder-meier first conceived of suicide parlors: he was growing ear-shaped. At least the top half of him was growing ear-shaped.

He noticed it late one winter afternoon as he was leaving his office. When he happened to look at himself leaving his office   in his raccoon coat & matching hat   in the wall-wide mirror he'd installed to the left of his desk, for patients to face themselves while they sat talking about themselves.

His patients rarely faced themselves. They'd have little need of him if they could face themselves. Their self-preoccupations were verbal rather than visual, at least for the 40 minutes they spent sitting across from him, murmuring/muttering/hissing/occasionally yelling their injured monologues.

The cumulative effect of which was beginning to deform his initially well-proportioned   & subsequently weight-controlled   torso.

He could see it clearly in the mirror   —delaying his departure from the office by 40 minutes; after removing his coat—:   the lengthening lobe of his stomach. The pinkish furl at the tip of his head. With a few illuminated hairs bristling around the shell. His initially well-boned face was caving into a canal, furrowed by years of listening to his patients' polyphonous complaints. & self-justifications.

68

Justified complaints, many times, about circumstances truly beyond their control. Unbearable circumstances which they kept attracting, & begged him to take away. To make bearable with the rainbow-colored pacifiers he held out to them, with scientific father fingers.

With Big Brother fingers, to younger male patients. Who often rejected his pacifiers. & his fingers. Demanding the real stuff. To stop the pain of living. To stop it all. Once & for all. Instead of anesthetized more-of-the-same tomorrows. Wishing that they were dead.

Before leaving his office that falling winter night, Dr. Biedermeier phoned an old friend, & asked her to meet him for dinner.

During dinner, he pushed his chair away from the table, & asked the old friend to take a close look: Did she notice anything out of the ordinary, something different, looking at him from the top down to where the table cut across his crossed knees?

The old friend wanted to know what it was she was supposed to notice: new jeans? It was hard to tell with him: he was always wearing the same   tight   uniform of the non-conformist. The knobby white sweater certainly wasn't new: she'd given it to him for Christmas a year ago. Did he want her to notice that he was wearing it?   Ah!   He had once again splurged on new frames for his glasses.

Dr. Biedermeier heaved a patient sigh & petulantly informed her that he was turning into an ear. At least the top half of him was turning into an ear. Couldn't she see it?

She couldn't. To her, Arnold Biedermeier was & always had been mainly a mouth.

He walked out on her over brandies, almost tempted to leave her with the check. He'd made a mistake, expecting a woman   even a professionally sensitive woman: a successful photographer of theater faces   to notice changes in a man's body. Few women looked at men as bodies. They mainly looked at men's social positions. It didn't seem to matter if the positions had unaesthetic torsos; and tweedy erections.

But he'd been afraid to go to his bar & expose a nascent ear to the sensitive eyes of the young men he met there. Who'd ignore him   or worse: might start reacting to him like women: to the affluent doctor rather than to: Arnie, who was practically one of their own cruisable selves; only slightly older; & richer   if they saw what he had seen in his office mirror.

Which he saw again   unmistakably   in his bathroom mirror when he got home from dinner. & again unmistakably the next morning, while carefully shaving along the upper curve of the external auditory canal. & again at 11 a.m., back in his office. When he sat down in his patients' chair, in an honest effort to face himself squarely.

Or rather: convexly & concavely. Not sure what color pacifier to hold out to the momentous ear he saw sitting across from him, above a pair of tight-jeaned legs, & ankle-booted feet. Anxiously peering through tinted Christian Dior glasses.

Framed in genuine-tortoise thoughts of suicide.

Which was readily accessible to him. Without pain, or bungling.

Unlike his patients, he had legal access to the real stuff, to end it all once & for all, if he so chose. If he chose not to face more-&-more-ear-shaped tomorrows.

At this point, facing himself in all honesty, concavely & convexly in his office mirror, he was struck by the enormity of his selfishness.

& of his professional incompetence: pacifying symptoms, but rarely able to remove the causes of his patients' complaints.

His humbled mind drew a blank. & was graced with a revelation. A timid smile dimpled the ear canal, as though god's little finger had suddenly loosened an obtuse bit of wax: Suicide needed to be made accessible to all of suffering humanity. Not only to doctors & dealers.

If people were offered a place where they could go to die

in peace, painlessly   perhaps even pleasurably   24 hours a day, 7 days a week, year-round, including holidays   —especially the suicidal holidays, such as Thanksgiving & Christmas—

thcy would bc alivc by their daily choice. & would have to stop complaining.

& he would be able to recover his former shape. A desirable shape, even by the sensitive standards of young men in bars, considering that he was 42.

Dr. Arnold Biedermeier acted on his revelation. He got on the phone & canceled his appointments for the day. Then he composed a concise proposal for the setting up of an experimental suicide parlor in New York City   to be followed by a chain of gvt.- or state-supported suicide parlors throughout the nation, if not the world   & mailed it to a former   dead   patient's husband, whose prominent public face he had saved from rumors of foul play a number of years ago, by testifying to the dead patient's recurrent suicide attempts.

Perhaps the   promptly remarried   widower would use his incontrovertible public weight to encourage the establishment of suicide parlors as one of the human services of the Department of Health & Human Services.

Dr. Biedermeier wrote eloquently about the right to self-destruction, as one of the true criteria of individual freedom in a civilized society. Instead of that society's insistence that individuals preserve themselves for unsolicited collective annihilation.

About freedom of choice, building individual responsibility for being, by being offered the choice not to be.

About quality of life as opposed to unimaginative suffering.

About the moral   & economic   questionability of enforced prolongation of painful, often unendurable existences.

For which his suicide parlors would offer not only a humanitarian solution, but a compensation. Something to look forward to: a personalized death, wish-designed to accommodate every conceivable ego image & fantasy.

Under the compassionate supervision of competent psy-
chiatrists. With the aid of competent anesthetists, nurses, secretaries, masseurs, priests (of all denominations), philosophers,
storytellers, theatre directors, musicians, visual artists, jugglers,
caterers, florists, & coffin makers.

Life-weary individuals could come & let themselves be
put to sleep painlessly. In peaceful privacy, holding an understanding hand. Or during a banquet, in the company of friends.
Watching or enacting a play. Or listening to music.

Dictating their memoirs.   Provided the dictation did
not exceed 24 hours: the death-wish-indulgence limit allowed
each registered applicant. During which time applicants were also
allowed to change their minds.

There were no other restrictions. Life-weary individuals
could come & poison/cut/stab/shoot/hang/ax/drown/club/stone/
burn/freeze themselves to death, with expert counsel & assistance. The parlor supplied all necessary tools & equipment.

If the gvt. took advantage of his proposal, & allotted the
funds necessary for its nation-wide realization, these multiple
services could be made available free of charge to every suffering
individual, & yet be to the gvt.'s earlier-mentioned economic
advantage.

Especially in view of the recent upsurge of age gangs,
composed of hollow-eyed senior citizens who had taken to the
streets of the larger cities since the discontinuance of their social
security checks. & were not only obstructing traffic with their
arthritic panhandling & shrill-feathered outdoor sleeping arrangements, but were also a demoralizing sight for taxpayers on their
way to work.

He trusted that his former patient's widower was still
gratefully remarried . . . & looked forward to . . . etc. . . . .

Dr. Arnold Biedermeier's eloquent proposal did not fall
on deaf ears.   —Deafness might have been another alternative;
but a selfish one.—   However, the gvt. saw little reason for
pampering refugees from life with a lavish death.Which would,

moreover, be wasted on the age gangs, that were composed of persons mostly beyond the age of sensory refinements. Their threat   though real enough with regard to traffic, & regrettably demoralizing   might perhaps be countered with more expedient, collective, egalitarian means.

Unfortunately one of the most expedient means had been regrettably discredited by a historical precedent, & rather than having recourse to it at this point in time, the gvt. deemed it wiser to let nature take its course: a roofless, food-scarce existence on winter city streets could not be overly conducive to longevity.

However: The gvt. would not stand in the reputed doctor's way, if he wished to try his experiment on his own & set up an initial suicide parlor in New York City. Preferably a less ambitious one, that would allow for an eventual emphasis on the afore-said less individualized, egalitarian   democratic   expediency. With best wishes . . . etc. . . . .

There was a check, signed by his former patient's obviously still grateful widower. A personal loan, convertible into an initial investment in the establishment of eventual, gvt.-supported chains of suicide parlors, if the first one caught on.

The check was large enough to acquire a burned-out building in a questionable neighborhood. To redesign the interior, & equip it with flexible facilities to accommodate the fantasies of 24 individuals during one 24-hour period. & to pay a modest salary to a small but dedicated staff. Of one: Dr. Arnold Biedermeier.

Who felt that he was answering a crying need.

But death   especially voluntary death   had been so successfully discredited in this complaining, blaming society that despite eloquent ads, & pep talks to the most miserable of his patients, only three candidates presented themselves on opening day. None of whom he knew. Two bums, & one bag lady.

The first bum looked 80, but insisted that he was 42, the same age as Dr. Biedermeier. When asked by what means he wished to die, he demanded a single room, & enough Bourbon to drink himself to death.

Although this demand exceeded the 24-hour death-wish indulgence limit, Dr. Biedermeier acquiesced. He was eager to get his project under way.

The second bum was in his late twenties, somewhat unkempt & emaciated, but still plausible as a body. He said that he used to be a writer, forced to earn his living as a proofreader for a textbook publisher. Who had fired him for inserting pertinent facts about Jefferson's sex life into a highschool history book. Since then he had been living by his wits, on a diet of coke & grass.

His wish was to die at the end of a meditation. To enter cosmic consciousness during a mescaline high, & then be finalized with a painless, imperceptible needle.

The bag lady, who refused to give her age, wanted to die like Cleopatra, with two vipers at her breast   (symbolizing her two daughters). After a bubble bath, a wash & set, a manicure, a pedicure, a steak dinner with wine, & a good night's sleep naked between satin sheets.

The next morning the old bum & the bag lady said they'd changed their minds about wishing to call it quits just yet, & stumbled out into the street like kids released from school, laughing & shoving each other.

Dr. Biedermeier was left with the young proofreader's still plausible, spaced-out body   —which would not have looked out of place in his bar—   propped against a wall in the lotus position. With vacant, pale-blue eyes.

With a sigh he sat down beside the body, & slowly crossed his legs. Which wasn't easy, in skin-tight jeans. He had brought two syringes, filled with the real stuff, precision-dosed according to body weight: 126 & 162 lbs. respectively.

He felt that his suicide parlor was everything he had promised: permitting an ear to die in the company of blue-eyed silence.

The Sin Eater

[for Andy Sisson]

THEY'VE ARRESTED ME for eating the baby. Which wasn't really a baby yet, a 6-month pregnancy that miscarried, killing its mother. After an abortion, which the mother performed herself. He never breathed, & he had not had time to commit any sins.

They've put me in jail for it. There are other women in the cell with me, but they moved away from me after I told them why I was put here. It doesn't bother me. I need to concentrate on digesting what I've eaten, to make it pass through me, to make sure I don't absorb it into my blood & take it on as sins of my own. Besides, I'm used to persons not speaking to me, or to anyone else in my family, except when they send for us when one of them has died.

My family has lived in Appalachia country for as long as anyone can remember. In a house that stands by itself on a slope, away from other houses. People treat us with respect, & they feed us well & plenty after they send for us. But they don't talk to us much.

That's why my brother Ron went away when he turned 15. Because nobody would talk to him in school, except the teacher. If he'd as much as smile at one of the girls she'd look away & cross herself. It bothered him enough not to want to stick around. That's how I came to take over for my father, when my father got too old to go to people's houses. Although it used to be the men in our family that took over the job.

But I know what to do. I have the tradition, watching my father do it until he got old: first you get called in to a place where someone has just died, & when you arrive they take you to the coffin on which they've laid out all kinds of foods: meat

vegetables   fruit   cheese   beer   wine   milk
coke   all kinds of stuff & plenty of it. They leave you alone, & you sit down & start eating.

We're known for neat eating, in my family. Still, some don't like it when I eat their deceased's sins in their houses. They're afraid something might crumble off & stay behind. So they pack everything up & make me take it home & eat it there. & some leave the coffin open, with the food piled all around it so I can get a look at the deceased, at the kind of sins he or she needs getting rid of most.

That's the way it was with Linda Mae, the woman whose sins I was eating when they arrested me.

Maybe I was being too conscientious. But I'd known Linda Mae. We used to sit in the same room in school with her, my brother Ron & I. She'd even smiled back at Ron once. & she used to be real pretty then, not all bloated & gray, the way she looked lying in that coffin. With the unfinished dead child forced into her arms, up against her bloated breasts.

I couldn't see her being buried with it lying on top of her   on her heart   after she'd killed herself getting rid of it. After her mother wanted to throw her out of their house, & her father said nothing, because the unfinished son inside Linda Mae was also Linda Mae's brother.

It was Linda Mae's father who'd called me in after his daughter died. But he said nothing when Linda Mae's mother had me arrested for eating Linda Mae's sin. Which was also the father's sin, more than Linda Mae's the way I see it.

I know I'll be out of here as soon as the judge understands why I did what I did.   —Which was disgusting to me besides.—   & I also know that I won't go to Linda Mae's house when they call me in when her parents die.

I sometimes wonder how my brother Ron is doing. Where he may be living. A woman I went to see before they arrested me, before Linda Mae died, who reads tea leaves, told me that Ron is working in a funeral home. Doing embalming. Doing real well with it, too. So I guess he stuck with the dead after all. I'm sort of glad he did. They're more reliable than the living.

Reassembling a Lady
Named Fred

THERE ARE THREE OF THEM NOW, combing through my clothes with acquisitive fingers: a pudgy brunette, somewhere in her thirties, a tall redhead with glasses, also thirtyish, & an older woman with a birdface & pale-yellow down for hair.

They're pinching the wools & silks & cottons, visibly impressed with the quantity & quality of my wardrobe, the international range of labels, of styles that date from the late twenties through yesterday.

They sound envious, speculating as to who I may have been: a performer   a retired international spy   an old-money heiress   a tycoon's well-kept secret/or guilt-etched wife. They decide upon the last: widowed, a traveled-out relic in a stately southern mansion.

They are less romantic about my body: Why does my waist measure 25 inches from the late-twenties through the late-thirties styles, & suddenly jump to 34 inches at the end of WW II, when decent people had been thin.

—At least decent people who had lived or dressed in France: according to the birdface who teaches history.

There is only one 34-inch-waist dress   electric blue linen with tight long sleeves, & buttons of the same material that start at the neck & run down the back to the mid-calf hem. I managed to move the buttons out by 9 inches, to accommodate

78

my 34-inch waist, during the one week it took to get my body
back to normal again.

—Hardly long enough to have been pregnant. Although that
is the suggestion of the redhead, who is measuring the electric
blue waist against her own. She could move back the buttons . . .

The pudgy brunette defends my political integrity: Perhaps I'd started over-eating as soon as the war was over   —
when I'd probably been young enough to have still been single.
The pudgy brunette is still single, though in her thirties.—   &
then dieted myself back into mating shape.

Maybe I'd been a GI bride.

& bow-legged? All my skirts seem to be mid-calf, even
when the short-shorts came into fashion. They're arguing about
my height: 5'7" (the redhead with the glasses, who is 5'6")
5'8" (the pudgy brunette, who is 5'4")   5'3" (the birdface,
who is also 5'3"). They decide that they can't decide.

They're disappointed because there are no shoes.

They're asking the long, thin-haired girl who's selling
my clothes if all these clothes belonged to the same person.
They're told that: yes, they did. They are the tail end of an estate.
But she can't   or won't   tell them whose estate it was. She's
just a volunteer: she says: Just helping out.

Obligingly she unfolds a green paisley dress   with jet
applique retracing the paisley pattern along the low square neck
    which the pudgy brunette wants to try on. Although she
hesitates when she sees the very short sleeves. She doesn't like
to show her arms.

She's right, of course; fat arms detract from the cut of the
neck, which is the main feature of this dress. But the other two
    & the long, thin-haired volunteer who's just helping out
convince her that she's wrong, & she disappears into a confessional stall, since my clothes are being sold in a church, to raise
money for the homeless.

I would have been well advised not to show my arms
either, when I first wore that dress, during my first unchaperoned

summer in Rome, although my arms never looked like nascent thighs, & during that summer I had an unfreckled even tan that set off the green & the glitter.

For the first time in my life I felt truly elegant as I left the *pensione* to set out on a reconnoitering stroll through the city. I had thrown away the sensible clothes I'd come with & spent my food money on the green paisley dress which the ill-advised pudgy brunette is trying on in the confessional stall   a white raw-silk coat which the birdface is pensively fingering (which I carried carelessly slung over one shoulder)   & matching green patent leather pumps with extremely high heels which are not included in the charitable tail end of my estate.

My room in the *pensione* had been paid for in advance. It included: one bowl of sugared milk coffee & 7 inches of buttered bread. It would do me good to live on nothing but breakfast for a week, & start looking interesting instead of healthy.

Like a sophisticated young woman at home in Rome, whose elegance distracted the onlooker from a very high, rounded forehead, at that time still conservatively devoid of bangs, which had earned me the unflattering nickname "Brains" from classmates who were getting even for copying my answers on Latin tests.

No sophisticated young woman at home in Rome would have gone walking in Trastevere on a Sunday morning. She certainly would not have gone alone, & she certainly would not have gone in a bare-armed, low-necked dress, even if the skirt was well below the knees. As was still the fashion then.

Exposing herself to shouts of: puta   puta. & to the sharp-edged stone that hit my upper left arm, spoiling my even tan with a months-long green & purple bruise.

I knew that running invited pursuit. Besides, I couldn't have run very fast in those high green heels. It occurred to me to take my shoes off, to make myself look more on a level with the barefoot stone-throwing teenagers in this neighborhood.

From which I needed to escape as fast as I could. Except

that I hesitated to turn back, in the direction of the stone, & had no idea where forward would lead me.

I saw myself walking the sun-drenched cobblestoned streets for the rest of my life   a shoe in each fist, the high pointed heels sticking up, to serve as weapons   until my elegant clothes turned shabby, & I blended into my environment, & became the neighborhood puta, to feed my ill-washed body, which would become professionally diseased & rot away without any hope of ever making it back to the clean side of town.

Where Federico eventually led me, by the elbow of my injured arm.

He was a trim man with gleaming teeth, who walked with a cane, & when he first came limping toward me, I thought it was to ask my price. Or worse: to enslave my virginal self through sex & then sell me to a whorehouse in Morocco. Which used to be a fear-fantasy among my female classmates.

Federico was   he said he was   a recently graduated architect from the Palermo school, whose specialty was the conception of more efficient penal & religious institutions.

He also was the most enjoyable guide I could have wished for, to show me Rome. He knew   or invented   a history behind every stone we passed.   —The toilet inside the sidewalk cafe he'd led me to had been part of a marble bench from Emperor Trajan's banquet hall.—   & was offering to show me around for the remaining five days of my stay. I accepted enthusiastically   —for that Sunday, but refused to see him after that. I didn't want him to discover that I owned only 1 dress / 1 coat / 1 pair of shoes.

The birdface has decided to buy my yellow Chinese housecoat. Despite the lumps in the quilting, caused by a rigorous dry cleaning. It's cheap, & she loves the deep egg-yolk yellow.

Which turned beige with dirt. & so stiff, it remained standing on its hem when I took it off, after the 78 days—the 1872 hours—I'd uninterruptedly worn it in jail.

Fresnes: the model prison of Europe, just outside Paris, which might have impressed my Roman Sunday guide with the efficiency of a toilet in each cell. Designed for a single inmate, but which the Nazis were packing with six men, or six women, during the last year of their occupation.

In my cell, the oldest inmate had been assigned the cot; the other five slept on straw mattresses on the floor. I was the latest arrival: my mattress was next to the toilet, my head touching the bowl.

—With an efficiency flush button inserted into the wall above the seatless porcelain rim. It was inserted so deeply that we had to use the ends of our spoons to make it flush.

June, July, & 17 days of August felt clammy inside the model efficiency walls in the crowded space.   —Which was anything but conducive to the mythologized "intimacies" with which people on the outside romanticize what they do to people on the inside.

Perhaps it was the ever-present fear that kept draining the warmth from my inactive body.   —Which bloated to a 34-inch waist.—   I was always cold, in my dirty quilted robe, every minute of the 1872 hours. Which felt unending, but shrank & ran together, once they had passed.

They'd double-lock our efficiency cell doors during air raids, & I'd lie   or sit cross-legged   on my dank straw mattress, imagining that the liberating bombs would neatly sever the walls, & we'd all step over the rubble, clothes-less perhaps, but free.

The pudgy brunette is walking around with a white silk turban on her head, in quest of a mirror. But of course there are no mirrors in the church. She doesn't trust the other two   or the long, thin-haired volunteer who's just helping out   who've been telling her how good it looks on her. This time they're telling the truth. She ought to buy it. Even if she doesn't get a chance to see herself first.

She thinks I must have had a pretty big head. Or lots of

hair. & that I'd probably worn the turban with the white raw-silk coat. Which she's also trying on. The birdface gave up on it.

Federico was wearing a white silk turban when I found him again when I returned to Rome for the first non-fascist fashion collection after the end of WW II.   —From which, I assumed, Federico had been exempted by his limp.—   He was sitting where I had left him, at the same table in the same sidewalk cafe with the imperial toilet, but dressed as a grand white-turbaned, white-kaftaned prophet, with an ivory-handled cane lying on the chair across from him.

He ignored my joyful smile of recognition, & gravely handed me a card. Which read:

Fredericus Sapius
By appointment only

in stilted gold letters.

I thought that my disguised friend was inviting me to join in some kind of game, & humbly requested to be granted an appointment with the great wise man. Miming exaggerated respect.

Which he ignored. He nodded gravely, removed his cane, motioned with it for me to sit down across from him, & to place my hands   palms up   on the cafe table between us.

Hm: he said. & again: Hm, frowning at my palms.

Which were beginning to sweat, under his silent unsmiling stare. I longed to see my friend's teeth gleam, to be let in on whatever game he was playing with me. But he just sat, staring at my palms.

Eventually he cleared his throat, & spoke. In a voice that seemed to come from an echo chamber at a great distance in time. We were: he said: the sum of various previous lives. Whose undigested experiences determined & explained the things that happened to us in this one.

My case was one of undigested pride. Of which the mechanics of reincarnation were reminding me by hitting me with flying objects. I was a magnet for flying objects, in expiation for having killed Frederick II, King of Sicily, Emperor of the Holy Roman Empire, with a flat, round, rock-hard bread. During a relatively recent   Sicilian incarnation. In Palermo. In 1250, when I'd put an end to 32 years of Frederick II's wise reign.

Frederick II had wanted me, but had not begged me enough. He had too readily accepted my indignant refusal. I had baked my bread with vengeance on my mind. I had let it grow hard   but not crumbly   & on the day which Sicilians consecrate to San Galogero, their rotund black saint, I had demurely stood at my kitchen window & aimed for the royal temple of my too readily resigned wooer. Who had graciously consented to being one of that year's statue bearers.

My bread had, however, caught Frederick II in the left royal knee pit. Which had caused him to buckle & trip. The heavy statue of the rotund black saint had fallen on top of him, & crushed him to death.

San Galogero's statue was still being carried through Sicilian streets during a yearly procession. While pious onlookers tossed bread from their windows or balconies, or ran up to the statue, to wipe the black-glistening face with kerchiefs that became stained with saintly black sweat, which they carried close to the skin, to ward off sickness & famine.

Sicilians were a frugal people, with a keen sense of thrift. It was common practice to save up stale bread for the San Galogero procession. & sometimes to aim for the legs & arms of the statue bearers, as a practical joke. Although, because of the royal presence during that particular procession, all breads but mine had been soft & fresh.

I'd been a scholarly young woman, with a fiercely virginal reputation. No one had suspected the dead king's strawfire passion for me. Onlookers had automatically assumed that they'd witnessed a freak accident, for which I'd received almost as much condoling & consoling as the widowed queen.

Who had cried in my arms.

& eventually persuaded me to move into her palace as her

constant companion & confidante, whose advice she'd ask & heed. I had lived a long, unrepenting spinster's life, smugly sleeping next to the widowed queen, in the canopied conjugal bed, in the place of my royal victim.

Taking the place of one's victim & assuming the dead person's obligations had once been a punishment for murder, accepted by certain tribes of American Indians. But I'd hardly been equipped to take on my victim's conjugal duties, even though the widowed queen had looked content enough, after I'd moved in with her. & I had made decisions   through her in matters of state.

However, this was not acceptable in Sicily, where customs required two eyes in replacement of one, & a full jaw for a single tooth. From a Sicilian point of view I'd been rewarded for my crime of pride. Therefore I needed to use this life for expiation. Or yet another life, if I missed my cue in this one. I would continue to be a target for flying objects   which would not kill me; merely tease me, with fear & minor pains   until I recognized the current incarnation of the king whom I had murdered with my bread. When I would be given the chance to digest my mechanical pride, by trading places for real.

I kept looking at the prophet's grave face, trying to lure my gleaming-toothed Sunday guide & savior out from under the grand white silk turban.   —Which the pudgy brunette has decided to buy, without the reassurance of a mirror.—   But he ignored my winking smiles & eyebrow action. & continued to stare at my upturned   sweaty   palms. Seriously cautioning me to avoid passing too close to tennis courts/walking through streets filled with ball-playing or rock-throwing teenagers/or under the windows of university dormitories. Whereas I had little to fear from: historically crumbling cornices/potted geraniums in window boxes/caving-in bathroom ceilings/or meteors. Which might lean dangerously close, but would ultimately crash a couple of feet away from me.

The prophet expressed surprise that no straying sniper's bullet had grazed my legs or buttocks, during the war.

Which he had spent in a monastery near Palermo, researching the role of chiromancy in medieval medicine. He had enjoyed the meditative life: he said: despite the initially disconcerting absence of mirrors.

I told him about Fresnes, the model prison of Europe, which had had no mirrors either.   —Which led to a brief discussion about the absence of mirrors in religious & penal institutions: Whether it helped or hindered facing the inner self.— & that there had indeed been three evenings of sniper bullets shortly before the liberation, courting my kitchen silhouette. But they were still embedded in the stone wall to either side of the Paris kitchen window.

The redhead with the glasses is in the confessional stall, trying on a wide-sleeved purple dress. It looks awful on her; I hope she's planning to change the color of her hair.

My concierge had worn that dress during my incarceration, never expecting to see me again. It was furtively returned to my closet after I came back. When I found it hanging on a hasty wire hanger, with large concierge-sweat moons under the arms. I wore it nonetheless, after I'd regained my freedom shape, waving wide-sleeved purple welcome to the liberating troops, on August 25, 1944, from my bullet-framed kitchen window.

At last the looked-for, longed-for smile gleamed at me from under the prophet's turban   —after I'd paid the prophet his   not modest   fee. Which he later spent on our dinner at Alfredo's. Where we twirled fettucine with golden forks & spoons.—   as he complimented me on my fall suit: a knobby brown knit, with a fluted skirt, still five inches below the knee, & brass- & brown-suede buttons.

For which: he said: I needed matching shoes.

The birdface has been coveting that suit, but so far she has acquired only the yellow Chinese housecoat: for 50 cents.

Perhaps she's poor. Or stingy; at least with clothes. Perhaps she spends all her history-teaching salary on improving her nest.

Unlike the pudgy brunette who wants to buy everything.

I told the now consistently smiling prophet that I had just bought the suit in Rome. Where I had come to see the fall collections. That I'd helped start a new designer in Paris, after the war, & that our house was dressing Gertrude Stein.

He enthusiastically accepted my invitation to accompany me on a tour of my Italian competitors. We spent a long afternoon looking at striking women parading striking clothes. Later he took me to a shoemaker   —after closing time; through the back door into the living quarters of the shoemaker—   who measured my feet for brown suede lace-up ankle boots. With the childishly rounded toes that were in fashion then.

& extremely high heels. Which: the prophet said: he envied women for wearing. But couldn't wear, even if he were a woman. Tapping his left leg with the handle of his cane. I looked down at the stiff black shoe protruding from his kaftan, & realized only then that he might be wearing an artificial leg. In my embarrassment I admired his cane: ebony, with a lively-eyed lion for a handle, chewing at its own outstretched paw, with gleaming teeth.

A symbolic reminder of his former self-destructive ways: the prophet gleamed: before he'd been given the chance to face himself, during the war, in the mirrorless monastery near Palermo.

We wound up the evening in my hotel room, drinking grappa over crushed ice, discussing the relationship of fashion to world events, whether fashion was their prophet, or merely their chronicler. & we agreed that fashion was prophetic. Perhaps because it had come into being as an image projection   & subsequent expression of power & office   of men & women who were at the top. Or wanted to give the impression of being at the top. Or being close to kings & queens, presidents & prime ministers, who made the decisions that made history.

Leading men & women whose dress & mannerism were imitated by the docile & the ambitious among their contemporaries. & contradicted by the rebellious ones. With bold stripes & "natural" hair, which had announced the French revolution.

We started parading around my hotel room, giggling, slightly drunk, imitating kings & queens staggering under the weight of crowns & gowns   corsetted courtiers, breathing sparingly with calculated care   hoop-skirted courtesans who had to turn sideways to sway through doors   ancient Romans & fashionable secretaries balancing their steps on cothurns & stiletto heels.

& we decided that we admired them for the discipline of their discomfort. Which we found as demanding as the mirrorless contemplation of the inner self.

We made a breakfast appointment for 9 the next morning at his sidewalk cafe with the imperial toilet, but neither the architect Federico nor the prophet Fredericus Sapius appeared during the two hours & twenty minutes I sat in front of a cappucino, checking every person that entered the cafe   & all the people who passed on the street   for gleaming teeth, & a cane, & a stiff black left shoe on a left leg that might have been amputated at the knee   in yet another disguise, perhaps. I finally left the cafe   & Rome three days later   without seeing my friend(s) again.

The sensible redhead with the glasses has decided against the purple dress. Not because the color looks awful on her, & she doesn't want to dye her hair, but because she has detected my old dead concierge's sweat moons under the arms. No amount of dry cleaning could remove them: they're still discernible, after exactly four decades.

Instead she's tempted to buy a black low-backed crepe de chine, with long clinging sleeves & a ruffle around the equally clinging skirt, 5 inches below the knee, & equidistant from the hem.

She should buy it. It was a bridal gown which climaxed our first New York collection. In which: The Bride Wore Black. It is beautiful & timeless. & it was worn only once.

By my friend Federico.

If the prosperous-looking gentleman who hailed me with gleaming teeth   from a sidewalk cafe in Little Italy *was* my friend Federico.

I was not expecting to run into anyone, during my first visit to New York City, least of all into yet another impersonation of the man who had led me from the threatening stones of Trastevere on a Sunday morning at the dawn of my elegance.

The pudgy brunette is taking the green paisley dress with the jet applique around the neck, despite its very short sleeves. She'll hide her arms in the white raw-silk coat, which she's also taking.

I was about to walk on   despite the gleaming teeth had the prosperous-looking gentleman not hooked the handle of his cane around my left knee. I nearly fell, & had to hold on to his table for support.

He quickly removed his foot from the chair across from him, motioning for me to sit down. With the ivory handle of his cane, for which he apologized as though it   & not he   had tripped me. He was still suffering from a long-standing injury to his left knee: he said: & couldn't walk too well without the cane.

I nodded, & patted the familiar lively-eyed lion that was forever chewing at its paw. I forgave it: I said, winking at the lion's owner. Waiting for a glimmer of recognition. An acknowledgment of continuity, leading back to our first encounter in Trastevere. But the prosperous-looking gentleman did not wink back, though his teeth continued to gleam. Politely. Expressing gentlemanly pleasure at making my acquaintance in a sidewalk cafe in Little Italy.

He was an art dealer: he said: who specialized in Sicilian folk art. Which I might or might not be familiar with. Lively scenes from operas or popular dramas, painted on the wooden back flaps of Sicilian donkey carts. He'd just flown in from Palermo with an exquisite collection.

He handed me a neat pile of slides   —on which primitive figures with raised arms seemed to be beating other figures with their hands to their heads, while still others lay prostrate on the ground—   which he hoped, & hated, to sell in New York.

He hated to let go of them: he said: He had derived great aesthetic & emotional satisfaction from collecting these donkey-cart paintings. Which were like mirages of his Sicilian past. But the time had come for him to let go of all the things that bound him to his past. Beginning with the pleasure-giving things, if he wished to be rid also of the painful ones.

I said that: *my* aesthetic & emotional satisfactions were derived from beautiful clothes. Of which *I* had brought a collection to sell in New York.

I asked if he would like to come up to my hotel room for a sneak preview since I had no slides to show him.

He accepted enthusiastically. Complimenting me on the silver suit I was wearing. Which was as beautifully simple, in its sophistication, as were his donkey-cart paintings in their primitiveness.

The long, thin-haired volunteer who's just helping out has set the silver suit aside for herself   under the red altar cloth, where she has also hidden the cane with the ivory lion handle   as her reward for helping out.

I had not expected Federico to express the desire to try on the clothes of my first New York collection which I was showing to him in my hotel room.

—If the prosperous-looking gentleman & art dealer from Palermo was the Roman architect Federico from the Palermo school of architecture whom I had first met on a Sunday morning

in Trastevere. & perhaps again as a sidewalk cafe prophet, who
had called himself: Fredericus Sapius. & who now bitterly resented being called: Fred, by the New York art dealers to whom
he was selling his donkey-cart paintings.—

I was not prepared to watch the art dealer step out of his
prosperous-looking suit.

Nor the firm, narrow model's body that emerged from the
prosperous-looking suit. & easily slipped into the striking skirt
& blouse. Which looked more striking on him than on the professional models I normally used.

Despite his injured left leg. Which seemed to become less
& less noticeable as he tried on more & more clothes. & seemed
to disappear altogether when he put on the black bridal gown.

The redhead & the birdface have paid for their clothes.
They're standing at the door of the church, waiting for the pudgy
brunette. Who can't see where she's going, from behind the stack
of clothes she has bought. Despite the weight across her outstretched arms she has a stately walk.

Rumors/Murky Haloes

A MAN-SIZED 16TH-CENTURY RAGDOLL sits smiling in a corner of my background, encased in family myth & gore. Leaking sawdust. Bearing testimony to the material existence of a legendary French executioner by the name of Denis, for whom Henry VIII allegedly sent, in 1536, to have him cut off the adulterous head of Anne Boleyn. Granting her the last favor of: a French executioner.   —Who became my ambiguous ancestor, thanks to the interference of a tavern owner's wife from Pau.

According to the family legend, the frail, pale-eyed Denis made his appearance in Paris around 1533   or 1534   as the official replacement of the old executioner, who had missed four necks in succession.

—Which a number of his neighbors didn't consider a sufficient reason for turning his stocky familiar figure   with a wife & four as-yet-husbandless daughters   out of the house behind the execution square (the present Place de l'Hôtel de Ville; since 1806) in which he had officially lived for the close to fifteen years that he had been enforcing 16th-century justice, in Paris. To make room for a lithe newcomer. Who had come out of nowhere. & didn't need two rooms to live in, alone.

The tavern owner's wife had the notion that the new executioner had come from Pau. Because of a windy way he had with his "h's." Where *she* had come from, seventeen years be-

92

fore, when she had been eight months pregnant with her daughter.

—Where pale eyes & pale hair had been his natural apprenticeship for an outsider's profession: according to some who thought that the new executioner was the best they had ever watched. & began to affirm that he had chosen his profession out of a dedication to humanity.

—Whose progress prudishly ignored the human breeding process, to focus instead on grafting trees & crossing mares with asses. While the quality of people was allowed to deteriorate.

Since the beginning of the century it had in fact dropped to a doom-level of depravity, which the new executioner was hoping to curtail: cutting off heads that had become depraved to the point of crime.

To which he did not wish to add the crime of sloppy workmanship   —unlike the old executioner—   meting out blunt or clumsy punishment. Which was why he kept perfecting his innate skill.   —Perhaps there lay an executioner on the groundfloor of our civilization, twitching like a city dog dreaming wildlife.—   & practiced at home; behind drawn curtains; on the neck of a man-sized ragdoll, stuffed with sawdust. Which he had brought with him   from Pau, or from wherever he had come.

Whose neck he painstakingly restuffed & resewed, after each practice decapitation.

Acquiring the reputation that was beginning to spread his name beyond the confines of Paris   beyond the borders of France: that his ax had a magic touch which allowed the about-to-be-executed to lay a trusting head upon the execution block, & concentrate on salvaging his soul.

A growing number of people began to affirm that the new executioner was a saint.   —Another Saint Denis, like the indisputably saintly first Bishop of Paris.—   That he had stripped his frail pale-eyed life of all the satisfactions other men lived for: living alone, without as much as the creature comfort of a housekeeper. Contenting himself with celibate tavern meals, which he ate at a table by himself, isolated behind the screen of awe which his profession & his steadily spreading fame drew around him.

—Always at the same window table that looked out on the execution square. (The former Place de Grève; until 1806.)

Others, who doubted the new executioner's saintly dedication to humanity   out of a distrust for anyone whose roots they could not lay bare   affirmed instead that the blasphemously named Denis lived alone because he hated people. Whose heads he enjoyed cutting off. Which was precisely why he had been appointed executioner of Paris.

—By the high-placed protector he obviously had.   —At the court? In the church?—   Who had obviously been trading favors: finding a niche for somebody's perverted son.   —Unless the perverted son happened to be the high-placed protector's own unavowable bastard.

—With the innate thirst for getting even that bastards grew up with.

Which had inspired the adolescent executioner's favorite game: cutting off the heads of dolls. Which he stole from a legitimate sister.

Which malicious tutors found   or fashioned   for him. Dolls, with faces that bore a malicious resemblance with the legitimate sister   a legitimate brother   with the disavowing protector.

Dolls whose faces were the boy-executioner's own creations. Which he tirelessly repainted & rearranged, to bear the features of his growing hatred of people. In preparation for cutting off their heads. (—Perhaps there lies an executioner at the bottom of creative imagination, hooded like a cobra dreaming apples.)

While anxious tutors stood & watched, apprehending the appearance of an unmistakable tutor face, under the unsettlingly skillful hands of their charge.

—Unsettlingly delicate hands, with exquisite almond-shaped nails on the fingers.—

After watching a number of executions, those who believed in the new executioner's high-born-bastard perversity began to challenge the believers in his saintliness to go inside the house behind the execution square   (the one-time Place de Grève; since 1806 the Place de l'Hôtel de Ville)   to see how the new executioner lived   alone   behind drawn curtains. But even the most determined curiosity hesitated at the sight of the two dogs that had suddenly lain on either side of the new executioner's door, one early morning. Two dogs that stood tall as calves   & quivering   when they jumped to their feet at the sound of someone approaching.

The tavern owner's wife felt that the dogs were meant for her, when she looked across the square from the tavern window that first morning, & saw them lying outside the new executioner's house.

Where she had been the afternoon before. & had seen his practice dummy.

But she hadn't told anyone what it looked like. Not even her husband.

She had only told her husband   & her daughter   that the new executioner didn't want a housekeeper, after she came back from his house.

The afternoon after his twenty-fourth execution, which the tavern owner's wife   or anyone else who had watched it   was not likely to forget. Because that was the first time anyone saw a head drop in the basket with a smile on the face.

Before they all grew used to the smile. & watched for it. & would have felt cheated without it.

The tavern owner's wife could not believe her eyes, at first, when she saw the smile form on the fear-congested face, in the growing morning light. When she saw the face relax the instant the ax touched the neck: as though the blade was transferring its lightning radiance to the buck-toothed mouth.

—Which used to grin into the nightmares of the tavern owner's wife   & perhaps into the nightmares of other women who had been raped by the man on the execution block. Seventeen & a half years before his execution, when the tavern owner's wife had been on her way up from Pau   by herself to join her husband in Paris. When she had been eight-months pregnant with her daughter.   —Who had grown up to be her husband's daughter more than hers.—   Which she had never told her husband, in case he said that she had asked for it.

It was because of the unbelievable smile   like relief spreading over the nightmare face on the execution block that the tavern owner's wife had gone to the new executioner's house, finally. To appease her daughter, who had been crying to keep the new executioner's house since the evening he first walked into the tavern. A clammy March evening, in 1533. Or 1534. But she waited until afternoon, in case the executioner slept, after an execution.

—She thought that he must still be sleeping when he didn't answer her knock. She quietly opened his door, & tiptoed inside: into a dark unfurnished room, with only thick curtains before the window. Where she paused, smiling to herself, thinking that the new executioner could certainly use a woman's hands   her daughter's   to bring a little creature comfort into his empty life. Before she tiptoed on, into the next room. Which looked less dark   —unless she was getting used to the curtained twilight that was not unlike the pale morning light of executions—& had a straw bed on the floor. & one chair in the window corner.

On which the new executioner was sitting   completely motionless   still wearing his official execution robe, but without the hood. The ax gleaming on his motionless knees.   — Smiling the same blissful smile she had seen come to the nightmare face early that morning.

The tavern owner's wife smiled back at the seated executioner. Timidly; respectfully asking if he could perhaps use a housekeeper.

To which the seated executioner made no reply. But continued to sit, motionless & smiling. At her, standing there, praising the qualities of her daughter.   —Thinking: what a frail, small-boned man he was, for a man of his profession.

Suddenly, his voice had been behind her back, thanking her politely. Nearly scaring her out of her skin.

When she spun around, she found herself face to face with another executioner. Who was standing. Not wearing his robe. & not smiling. At her, standing transfixed, looking from the unsmiling face back to the smiling face in the window corner. & back.   —Making her feel like an utter fool when she realized that she had been offering her daughter's services to his practice dummy.

When an eery feeling crept over her, with the realization that the practice dummy looked exactly like the new executioner. Except that the dummy was smiling, & the new executioner was not.

& the tavern owner's wife asked herself what kind of man the new executioner was   if he was indeed a saint   to be cutting off his own head in daily practice.

—Except on days of executions. When he cut off the heads of criminals.

—To whose criminal faces he transferred the release-smile from the dummy's face.

& she continued to stand transfixed. Wondering if the new executioner would stop practicing, now that he had succeeded in transferring the smile.

Or if he would continue to practice, because he could never be sure that he could do it again. & again; every time. To every criminal face that lay before him on the execution block.

When a wave of compassion washed over her   almost washing her away   as she stood looking into the new executioner's polite blank face, to which he had not been able to transfer the smile.

& she wanted to kneel to the new executioner, & kiss his hands   —which looked surprisingly frail, for a man of his profession; more delicate than her own; with beautiful, almond-shaped nails on the fingers—   but the new executioner had placed one frail-looking hand under one of her elbows, & was steering her out.

Back through the empty thickly curtained room. To his as-yet-dogless front door. Where he thanked her once again for her concern. With blank politeness. Assuring her that he needed no one. No one.

Which was all the tavern owner's wife told her husband & her daughter, when she returned to the tavern.

Which made her daughter cry. Because her daughter was sure the new executioner was keeping a mistress who was keeping his house for him.

But the tavern owner was sure the new executioner was impotent. Which he wanted no housekeeper to find out.

Which made his wife wonder if women had perhaps been cruel to the new executioner. Before he came to Paris   —from Pau; if he did come from Pau, where women   people   had seemed to be less cruel than in Paris.—   If that was why he lived alone.

& her daughter cried more. Because she was sure she could cure the new executioner's impotence, if only he let her be his housekeeper.

But the tavern owner didn't want his only daughter going into the house of an impotent man. Who was trying to get even, cutting off the heads of other   potent   men. Who died laughing at his impotence, like the last one that morning.

& his wife began to say prayers in her head, for the new executioner, because it was occurring to her that the new executioner had killed the woman who had been cruel to him. When she mocked him when he came to love her, in his impotence.

—& that it was the woman's mocking smile he kept cutting off   together with his head   in daily expiation.

—Except on days of executions, when he cut off the heads of other murderers. Which he did, however, not sew back on.

—Except that the smile on his practice face was a blissful smile. Of redemption.

Lying in bed that night   close to the edge of the bed she shared with her husband   the tavern owner's wife found herself wondering what it might be like to lie with an impotent man. Quietly. In his arms; holding one of his delicate hands. Without the nozzle of potent desire pushing into her, regardless of whether she was open or not.

The next morning, the two dogs had lain on either side of the new executioner's door. & she had felt that they were meant for her, as a warning not to come offering him any more services.

Before the rumor began to circulate that: the new executioner had unnatural relationships with his dogs.

A rumor which seemed to be confirmed   —No wonder!—   when he took the dogs to England with him, in the spring of 1536.

When people rushed to his house. & were surprised to find his door wide open. As though he had expected them to come rushing. Making them practically fall into the first   completely empty   room. Where they found nothing but thick curtains in front of the window. Where they caught their step, before they strolled into the second curtained room. Where they found only a straw bed on the floor. & one chair in the window corner.

To which the tavern owner's wife had rushed ahead of the others. To get hold of the practice dummy before anyone else saw that it looked exactly like their new executioner. Like his twin, except for the smile.

But he had also taken his practice dummy with him to the court of England.

—Where he had allegedly refused to go, at first. Refusing to cut off the head of a woman. Until Anne Boleyn herself beseeched him. Sending him a miniature of herself which exposed her small slender neck. Which she trusted no one but him not to miss. Trusting no one but the French executioner not to send her running   headless   around the execution block. Making a spectacle of herself, before Henry & his new bride.

—Neither of whom   nor anyone else among the watching English courtiers   saw if Anne Boleyn died with a smile, because of the hair that was falling over her face. Because she had lifted her hair from her small slender neck   with her twelve fingers   when she laid her head on the execution block.

—When the French executioner's ax had raised itself, as though by reflex.

The executioner looked changed   fatter   to the tavern owner's wife, when he returned from the English court, two seasons later. With his two dogs. &   —she assumed   —his dummy.

—Unless he got rid of the dummy in England, when he learned to smile.

At the reddish-haired English apprentice he was bringing with him.   —For whom he had perhaps traded his dummy?—

Who ate with him at the window table. & smiled back at him, with long teeth. Which reminded the tavern owner's wife of the buck-toothed rapist. Which made her shudder when she accidentally touched his hand, handing him his plate. When she noticed the reddish hairs between the knuckles of the apprentice's long bony fingers. Which were lying on one of the executioner's forearms, as he talked.

—In a funny-sounding French which made the executioner smile more.

Which made the tavern owner's daughter giggle, every time he said something.

Until the rumor began to circulate that: the executioner had an unnatural relationship with the reddish-haired English apprentice. Which was not surprising: the English being what they were.

When the tavern owner's daughter began to cry: because she had fallen in love with the reddish-haired English apprentice since he had first walked into the tavern behind the returning fatter-looking executioner.

—Who also looked paler to the tavern owner's wife. Who thought that the food he had eaten at the English court couldn't have been very good, to have put so much weight around his middle. Making him look like a fat monk, when he stood behind the execution block in his official robe.

Which wild hands were tearing off the executioner's back, one chilly early execution morning. Just as the tavern owner's wife was about to sit down at her window table, preparing herself to see yet another smile of redemption appear on yet another criminal face.

Unprepared to see   her daughter's   wildly tearing hands expose the shrunken-soft belly of a recently delivered woman, in the growing morning light. A naked woman's body, with the executioner's hood over the head, that stood shivering behind the execution block, protecting milk-swollen breasts with frail-looking hands.

Before it teetered, & fell to its knees, as dozens of wild hands forced the hooded head down on the execution block.

—Her daughter's hands prominent among them.—   To the rhythmic chanting of: De—nise   De—nise—

When the tavern owner's wife gagged at the realization that she had been in love with a woman, for the past two years. Or longer. Ever since the afternoon after the first smile, when she had offered her daughter's services to the dummy.

De—nise   De—nise   De—nise   De-nise.

Gagging at the sight of her love's unknown body being put to death. Clumsily. By a shaking ax, which the wild hands were forcing into the shaking hands of the reddish-haired apprentice. Forcing his bony fingers with the reddish hairs closed around the handle. Raising his wildly shaking arms.

When the tavern owner's wife flew out into the square. Through the increasingly frantic chanting of: De—nise   De—

nise. Past her daughter's wriggling back. Propelled by the thought that the unknown body of her love had given birth to a child. Which the wild hands had perhaps overlooked, in their frenzy.

Although they had not overlooked the dogs. Whose two headless bodies lay on either side of the wide-open door.

Through which the tavern owner's wife flew. Through the curtained empty front room to the straw bed on the floor in the second room.

—Where her love had lain with the reddish-haired apprentice: which made her wince. Where she found the naked practice dummy lying   smiling   on top of a recently born male child. That was close to suffocation.

Which the tavern owner's wife took into her arms, & carried off to Pau. Together with the dummy that bore the features of her love.

Eye witness accounts of beatific smiles appearing on the faces of persons about to be executed abound since the beginnings of capital punishment. An implication of redemption, to redeem the spectacle of legislated murder.

& it is an undisputable fact that my frail, pale-eyed twin brother Dennis stole one of my ragdolls. Whose face he repainted & rearranged until it looked like me. Or like himself   —Except for its ineradicable ragdoll smile.—   Before he gave it back to me: in two pieces. After he cut off the head.

Shadowplay on Snow

I'VE BEEN SLEEPING WITH my great-grandmother's left thigh bone under my pillow since my seventeenth birthday, when my father gave it to me "to fend off potential dormitory rapists." I can hold it at the knee end & swing it like a club.

So far I've had no occasion to use it. & I don't expect to have the occasion as long as El Saint & I stay together. He's a vegetarian who took refuge in the Buddha four years ago, but he's typecast as the leader of a streetgang. They undressed him, at the customs, and made him take out his earring   —which they dunked into an acid-smelling lotion, to make sure it wasn't hollow—   the night we flew back in from Brazil, dizzy with exhaustion after eight hours of watching obscene cloud formations. They couldn't believe he wasn't carrying *something*.

El Saint freaked out, the first time he slept in my bed, when he put his arm under my head under the pillow, & his hand encountered the bone.

He sat up all night, looking at it. Turning on to what he calls: the elegance of functional shape. My great-grandmother Molinaro has become his guru. He rubs lemon oil into her thigh bone, & meditates in front of it.

Visualizing the flesh back on around it, I sometimes suspect. The smooth flesh of her late twenties, as he pictures my great-grandmother Molinaro's left thigh in her late twenties, sometime between 1865 & 1870, when she came to America to marry beneath her.

To absolve her intelligence from the exquisite-amateur status which the nineteenth century reserved for the minds & talents of well-born women: according to my mother. Who is convinced that my great-grandmother Molinaro hoped to gain intellectual independence by marrying a man who wouldn't be able to use her intelligence as a discreet backdrop for his position in the world. Marrying a social "inferior" may have looked like a promise of equality to an intelligent   perhaps not overly realistic   nineteenth-century woman.

According to my father: my great-grandmother had fallen in love with Amilcare Baltassare Molinaro, at close to thirty. & Amilcare Baltassare Molinaro had fallen in love with her. Which made them equals.

—Which had suddenly made the well-born woman realize that her mind was not located in her head, as she had been led to assume for close to thirty years. That it was located slightly to the right of her heart, "where Amilcare Baltassare Molinaro had touched the center of her being with his warm weathered hand": as she wrote in an undated eleven-page-long letter to someone named "Anne."

Which she must have written shortly after her arrival in America. She is still looking at herself with the eyes of her former life. Winking at herself, perhaps for the sake of "Anne" who was not close enough to be a confidante, but mattered enough to deserve an explanation. A justification.

Which she never sent, finally. Or perhaps copied, or re-wrote, after rereading it herself. When she had perhaps doubted that "Anne" would have much sympathy for her realization that she had "cheated her intelligence for close to thirty years, playing the demoiselle Agnès de Beaujeu, in sleepwalk subservience to the rules & regulations of society."

Which had reminded her for close to thirty years that she belonged to a family that had produced a *régente,* some four

centuries earlier. The able, energetic Anne de Beaujeu: 1460 to
1522 . . .

—When it had conceivably been less unthinkable that a
demoiselle   de Beaujeu; a *régente*   invited the son of the
family's Italian head gardener to her bed . . . : as she wrote to
"Anne."

Apparently quoting from a conversation she'd had with
her parents a number of months before she decided to leave for
America   (which had perhaps made her decide to leave for
America)   when her mother had apparently expressed the unsuspected opinion that "women   at least well-born French
women   had conceivably enjoyed greater freedom   at least
tacitly   in the days of the family *régente*.

"When the consequences of the *régente*'s indulgence in
her fondness for the people might conceivably have been placed
with a suitable couple, that would have appreciated the honor as
much as the additional income.

"When she might have had her indiscretion discreetly
tutored, until early manhood or early womanhood, when a minor
title might have been bestowed upon the bastard, depending upon
the mother's rating at that particular political moment in time.

"& upon the bastard's wit &/or beauty. Both of which
could occasionally be quite remarkable, in the case of bastards.
Which was one of the classical jokes nature was fond of playing
on human laws. Which was why the people in the understanding
of their simple hearts called bastards: 'natural' children, as opposed to unnatural legitimate ones." . . .

Which had greatly surprised my great-grandmother. Im-
plying unsuspected resignation in her mother's life; a quenched
rebellion in her mother's past. About which she cautiously ques-
tioned "Anne," who had "known [her] mother longer" than she
had.

Which had apparently made my great-grandmother's
father raise his hands in a gesture of "fatigued finality." & say
"in a tone that matched the gesture" that, even though his wife

seemed to hold the privileged opinion that her position in society
was inversely proportionate to social progress, he trusted that she
would nonetheless concede that it had been as inconceivable in
1485 as it was inconceivable today   (around 1865 or 1870)

that a de Beaujeu   —of either sex   —seriously considered
sharing the necessary, certainly; & by all means praiseworthy life
of an Italian gardener's son . . .

Who would promptly grow into an Italian garden toad,
under her repentant eyes. While she tried to do the things that
had been done for her all her former life.

Which she did badly, to the toad's growing disgruntle-
ment, because she had not been taught to do things with her
hands.

—Except to paint. Which she did remarkably well. Perhaps too remarkably, for a demoiselle who was ill advised to take
her pastimes seriously.

& to play the spinet. Which she might try to play a little
more remarkably, for the occasional entertainment of her family
& friends.

—Which was also   more or less   what the gardener's
son's mother said to her, after the gardener's son convinced my
great-grandmother to go to America with him, "where birth was
allegedly less important that what one did with it," & so the
Italian son wanted his mother to bless them both before they left.
On a moonless night in June.

In the long undated letter to "Anne" she describes how
she sat in the mother's "smoke-fogged" kitchen, where the
mother was curing freshly stuffed pork sausages.

With the help of a daughter   Celestina   who looked
"shockingly" like her brother. "A shockingly coarser replica of
the brother's Roman features. The same large heavy-lidded eyes,
but dull, whereas the brother's glowed with intelligence."

For the first & last time Agnès sat beside the mother
after the mother consented to sit, in the presence of the demoiselle, next to the demoiselle on the   probably pork-greased
kitchen bench.

Which the mother kept wiping with her heavy black cotton skirt, her eyes intent on the red-glistening movement of her hands which kept circling the empty space on the other side of her, while she said   to her hands   that: her son had always been taught to know his place. Which was not in the bed of a demoiselle. Who wouldn't know what to do with a gardener's son after he got out of her bed. & needed food. The demoiselle hadn't been taught to feed a husband. Or herself.

Not to speak of the child. Children, which noble ladies often started bearing at an age   at close to thirty   when the women of the people did their best to stop.

She didn't want to become the grandmother of little starvelings whom she'd be hearing whimpering in her ears day & night. All the way across the accursed water her son was fool enough to want to put between himself & his own: the mother said. Slowly detaching her eyes from her hands. Looking sideways/up at the tip of the demoiselle's nose.   —Which Agnès thought   might have been quivering slightly . . .

She'd be offending the Lord if she blessed her son's folly: the mother said: The Lord had not intended that kind of marriage, or He wouldn't have created idle people & working people, so that each found his place. Nobody could change the Law of the Lord, which was why revolutions always ended right where they had started: with the not-working at the top . . .

But the mother did bless her son, eventually. Because she didn't want to add to her son's hard-earned misery by withholding a mother's blessing.

& eventually she blessed even the demoiselle. With averted eyes. Because her son insisted that his mother bless his future wife. In Italian. Because his future wife knew Italian. Of which he   the son of Italians   knew only a couple of words in babytalk. & even those in the dialect of Rome. Insisting that his future wife "say something in Italian" to his mother.

& after a smoke-filled silence the mother stood up & called her daughter Celestina over, & said that she & her husband had lived in the expectation that their children would take care of them when they got old. As they were getting. But that they would accept losing their daughter as well as their son, for the sake of their son's survival in America. At least her son should take his twin sister Celestina to America with them.

—Which couldn't cost more than one of the sapphires out of the demoiselle's necklace. Which a gardener's wife couldn't have much use for, even in America.—

At least Celestina would know how to feed & clothe his family. Celestina had stuffed the sausages they were curing. Celestina knew how to kill a pig. & to set a hen up on her eggs so that she stayed put & hatched.

But Celestina had a fiance, & didn't want to become an old maid   the maid of her brother's wife   in her brother's house in America.

& when the demoiselle stood up to leave, her eyes tearful from the bitter kitchen smoke, the mother thought that she was crying.

Which emboldened the mother to say   in a new voice, without a trace of deference; the voice in which Agnès de Beaujeu expected to hear herself spoken to, in her new American life   by all but her husband   that she'd be wise to do her crying now, while there was still time. Because her son could always come back home, after he came to his senses, but his wife could not. Because the dead didn't come back, except as ghosts.

Because her noble family would declare that she had died   of indigestion   as soon as they found out that she'd run off with the son of their head gardener.

Her noble family would hold a mock funeral for her, & set up a mock monument with her name on it. & if she reappeared, they'd make sure that she became a ghost for real.

There was still time to throw herself at her parents' feet & confess: the mother said. It wouldn't be the first time that a de Beaujeu had farmed a bastard out for adoption.

Maybe Celestina would be willing to pass it off as her

own, for a small *pension,* & then the demoiselle could watch her own grow up. Which was all she had been taught to do: watch.

Looking charitable every time she gave Celestina's child a pair of shoes. Or an education. & nobody would be the wiser.

There was also a way to get rid of her bastard before she got big. With a goose quill. Which the mother might have been willing to put in place so that enough air got in   for a small compensation; for less than a sapphire   except that the mother couldn't be expected to make an angel out of her son's own . . .

But pregnancy wasn't my great-grandmother Molinaro's problem when she walked out of her former life, on the moonless June night, between 1865 & 1870, "carrying nothing but a few jewels to sell in Paris for the voyage . . . in a common-looking sack at which no thief would look twice"   still according to the unsent letter to "Anne"   "& her beloved [cat] Ménine." . . .

My great-grandmother came to America on one of the first steamboats of the compagnie générale transatlantique, the *Lafayette.* Which "accommodated only first- & second-class passengers, but sometimes   exceptionally   accepted up to twenty-seven men-only in the hold, without bedding." . . .

Among them my great-grandfather, who had "insisted on saving the sapphire necklace." . . .

The captain of the *Lafayette* married my great-grandparents on the eleventh day of their crossing, four days before they landed in New York.

Where they "were made to pass through a one-time amusement hall called Castle Garden. Where local merchants came to inspect the emigrants   like cattle, like slaves   to see whom they might have use for." . . .

My great-grandfather was offered work as a stonecutter, & they decided to stay in New York.

—"Where cats were surprisingly scarce."

After the birth of my twin grandaunts Celeste & Hermione "that dear Ménine earned a fine flannel blanket as good as new" for the babies, mousing for a Swiss neighbor on Greenwich Street. Where my great-grandmother kept a "summarily clean house." Whenever possible with the help of neighbors' wives who "could do in half a morning what would have taken [her] two days to do less well," in exchange for letters she wrote for them, in French or in Italian. Sometimes in German or in English.

The neighbors were usually "surprised & a little distrustful" when the stonecutter's wife sat down & wrote their letters for them at their dictation. Which "often embarrassed them, obliging them to reveal concerns or expectations which they ordinarily took pains to conceal."

My great-grandmother also designed some of the tombstones my great-grandfather cut. "The dead were affording them quite a good life," when my great-grandfather fell gravely ill, because "marble dust had seeped into his lungs." He had to give up stonecutting, & they decided to try growing white wine & follow a Swiss neighbor to Naples, Upstate New York. Which didn't officially become Naples until 1894.

Where my great-grandfather changed his name from Amilcare Baltassare to John. & where my grandfather Charlie was born in 1888.

According to my grandfather Charlie his mother had no regrets, & never wrote to her side of the family. But my grandfather Charlie was nine years old when she died   toward the end of the long winter of 1897/1898   & may have felt guilty for having survived her.

I never knew my grandfather Charlie. Or my twin grandaunts. Who remained unmarried, & went to France for a visit after my great-grandfather's death, when they were in their late fifties, & never returned to America.

Whereas my grandfather Charlie transferred his love for his mother to his country   in my mother's opinion   & had no use for anything that was not American.

It was from him that my father inherited the thigh bone.

My great-grandmother Molinaro did write   at least
fourteen   letters to her husband's twin sister Celestina. Who
kept her letters in a chipped marble mortar. In which they were
still being kept by one of Celestina's granddaughters when my
father read them after he tracked the granddaughter down, when
he was in France during & after World War II.

The letters to Celestina inspired most of the bedtime stories my father used to tell me when my mother was out of town.
They changed from fairytales to footnotes to history as I grew
older, & my great-grandmother Molinaro evolved from a fairy
princess into an intellectual rebel who thought she could beat
society by turning herself into a late nineteenth-century working-
man's wife.

Celestina's answers have been lost. But my father rein-
vented them in his stories. In which Celestina's character fluctu-
ated between affection & malice, depending on the annoyance-
level of my father's day at the private secondary school at which
he still teaches   on how he felt about the news   or about
my mother being out of town. Earning more in a week of lectures
than he was able to earn in five months of "attempting to provoke
an original thought in the congenitally conformist future heads
of corporations."

Some evenings Celestina was the loyal accomplice who
persuaded her fiance to drive my great-grandparents to Paris,
through the moonless June night.

Who sewed the thief-proof jewel sack. & took off her
heavy black cotton dress which she made my great-grandmother
wear over an easily recognizable gray-&-white-striped muslin
skirt & blouse.

But as my mother's lecture tours became more frequent,
Celestina became greedy. She demanded the sapphire necklace
as payment for the drive to Paris, or for her dreadful dress which
reeked of sweat, or for her sullen silence.

When my great-grandfather fell ill, Celestina had always
known that Agnès & America would be the death of him. But
when they moved to Naples, my mother cancelled her next lec-

ture tour, & Celestina became her initial loving self who felt that her brother's life would right itself now that he was working with the earth again.

It is altogether possible that my great-grandmother felt or was criticized by Celestina. & that she used Celestina's answers to light "the fine Dutch tile stove, white with blue corners" which was "most comforting to lean against in winter time," which they bought during their fifth winter in Naples, as she wrote in one of her fourteen letters.

Or perhaps my great-grandfather destroyed his sister's answers, because he felt that they were still hostile to his wife. Whose life was brave enough, with three children in an isolated half-finished farmhouse at the foot of a young vineyard, in the snowbelt of Upstate New York.

My great-grandmother Molinaro's last letter is dated October 28, 1897. Five months before she died, toward the end of an unusually long winter.

During which they ate all their rabbits & chickens. & the foxes that had come to the chicken house. Their goat. The deer that had come to their windows in search of food at the beginning of the snowfalls. Their emaciated dog which they could no longer feed. Four of their five cats; the fifth cat hid out somewhere & reappeared ghost-like after the snow began to melt. & several crows: according to my grandfather Charlie. According to what my father told me my grandfather Charlie had told him.

My father's voice always became shrouded in mystery when his story reached my great-grandmother Molinaro's death. It was not before I was thirteen   maybe fourteen   & asked: What exactly she had died of; if she had starved to death? that my mother told me that my great-grandmother Molinaro had committed suicide.

In my mother's opinion, my great-grandmother Molinaro felt that nature was allying itself with society against her, during the winter of 1897/1898. Proving to her what an inadequate housewife she was. & always would be. Who hadn't stored enough food to feed her family. & was responsible for their hunger. & would be responsible for their death. She had been gambling with the lives of others, in order to escape the role society had assigned her.

One night in March she crept from her bed & went to lie down in the snow behind the chicken house. Where she put herself to sleep with two bottles of my great-grandfather's cough medicine.

I've read the note she left on the kitchen table. In which she urged her husband & children to eat her, lest she "have died in vain."

"I can feed you better dead than alive," says her note. "You MUST eat me, to appease my soul."

According to my grandfather Charlie, starving foxes & rodents   perhaps also the missing fifth cat   had gnawed all the flesh off his mother's bones by the time they discovered her behind the chicken house. They found only her clean skeleton, still partly clad in a gray-&-white-striped flannel housecoat.

—Without her left thigh bone. Which my great-grand-father picked up a couple of hundred feet up the road to the vineyard, a month or so after the snow melted away.

By then they had buried her skeleton, & my great-grand-father kept her thigh bone & slept with it under his pillow until he died.

El Saint thinks my grandfather Charlie lied to my father. Unless my father has been lying to me. El Saint thinks that my grandfather Charlie   & the others   ate my great-grandmother Molinaro, & that she sustained them until the snow melted, & they were able to go in search of food. He refuses to believe that his guru died in vain.

He has bought me a gray-&-white-striped turn-of-the-century muslin skirt. I've noticed a new expression   like gourman-dise   around his vegetarian's mouth when he burrows into it to kiss my thighs.

Sweet Cheat of Freedom

[for John Evans]

HE HAD *NOT* SAID: No man is truly free until he has a slave.

No Roman feels free unless he has a slave: was what he had said   rather imprudently, perhaps   to the only daughter of his former master. The senator. When the senator had still been his master. Officially as well as *de facto*. Whose only daughter he had tutored for 11^{1}/$_{2}$ of her 16   almost 16^{1}/$_{2}$ years.

Had begun to tutor nearly twelve summers ago. After the senator became senator, after the death of his senator-father-in-law. When the new senator had decided   with his newly inherited rank   that he wanted his only daughter to grow up to think like a man. & had acquired a Greek thinking slave   from Sparta   to tutor her to grow up to think like a man. Like the son & heir to the senate he'd been prevented from having, by whatever it was he had given to his wife.   —Who was of better Roman birth than he was.—   Whatever it was he had brought home to Rome from the campaigns in southern Gaul, & passed on to his better-born wife, before he became senator after the death of his senator-father-in-law. Before he & his better-born wife began to age.

Before he began to resent his equally   but differently   aging wife. A little more each day. For not aging the way he was aging: rather resentfully; obesely. For cheating on nature.

By looking younger   & younger   than the one year that she
was younger than he was. Because of whatever it was he had
passed on to her, perhaps, that was perhaps delaying the natural
aging process of her 39-   almost $39^1/2$-   year-old better-born
body after preventing it from bearing him other children. Cheating him out of a son, after bearing the only daughter.

Who had grown up to resent her mother.

The senator's 45-year-old Greek   Spartan   thinking
slave liked to attribute the better-born wife's barely perceptible
    rather serene   aging to thinking. Which had perhaps been
prompted in her better-born mind by whatever it was that she
might have heard him say during much of $11^1/2$ years of daily
attempted dialogue in which he had tried to involve the only
daughter.

Who had perhaps resented her mother's almost daily presence, during much of $11^1/2$ years. From the first day on, perhaps.
Walling herself in willful stony deafness against whatever it was
that he might be saying.

About a little girl, for instance, who chose boredom in the
belief that she was choosing freedom.

Who was probably too little to understand that the only
true freedom was freedom of thought.   —Which many grown-
up Romans didn't understand either. Ever.—   For which one
had first to learn how to think. Not necessarily like a man. Or
like a Roman. But like a human being. The only true hierarchy
was, after all, a hierarchy of minds . . .

Some minds were better born than others. Not socially
better born, necessarily. Although a comfortable social position
    of senator parents   could be helpful in certain cases. Wasn't
always helpful, however. Induced smugness, laziness, & subsequent boredom, in certain cases.

Some beings arrived in the world better equipped than
others. With a head-start, so to speak. Which made it easier for
them to reassemble   in detail   the knowledge which the
gods took away from man in exchange for his first breath.

Man's first breath wiped his memory slate clean of most

of the subconscious total knowledge of life which he shared with
the gods up to the moment of his birth.

Continued to share with the gods in his dreams, after his
birth. When taking shape   taking on a specific—the human—
form   restricted man's grasp of life as a totality to the human
experience of life. To his own personal perception.

Which was his tool.

Which he had to use consciously   every day of his
life   in order to understand his relationship to other specific
forms of life around him: other men   animals   plants
mountains   rivers   the sky   the earth.

To understand all of life by means of his own specific life,
as he grew. Up. & older. Toward reabsorption by death. When
the gods judged by the sum total of his understanding whether
he had succeeded or failed.

Which failed to scale the willful deafness walls of the
$4^1/2$-5-$5^1/2$-6-etc.-year-old mind.

Which he continued to try to scale   unsuccessfully
for $11^1/2$ years.

Stealthily ignoring 7 to 8 years of boredom-born tantrums.

The subsequent recountings of which by the mother
amused the senator.

Until the tantrums gave way to an equally boredom-
born   equally deaf   passion for verbal disagreement.

Holding over 3000 monologues, while the only daughter:

Nudged her listening mother.

Tugged at her listening mother.

Poked her listening mother.

Climbed one of his legs.

Kneaded his lap with her toes.

Stared into his eyes.

Blew into his ears; his talking mouth.

Searched between his thighs with outrageous $4^1/2$-5-$5^1/2$-
6-$6^1/2$-year-old directness.

Which he   & the listening mother   tried not to see. To pay no attention to. On the principle that: what you don't feed cannot live.

On which principle   its positive & negative applications:

feeding an affection with attention—a mind with thoughts—a plant with water . . .

starving a resentment/a jealousy by withdrawing your thoughts from the subject/or object—an illness/a tantrum by ignoring it . . .

he continued to talk. While the mother continued to listen. Both conscientiously paying no attention to the only daughter.

Who disrobed. & marched out of earshot   past the patio confines of blue-clustering grapes   into the late-summer muck of the duck pond. In which she proceeded to roll her 5-year-old nudity until she was pulled out & returned to the patio   muck-crusted & flailing   by a weeping girl, a recent slave from southern Gaul, who was anticipating another beating   this one official, administered by the mistress of the house   after the unofficial one administered by painful bruising 5-year-old fists.

Which the mistress of the house did not administer. Had ceased to administer   to any of her slaves   after listening to one of his early monologues about the non-violence of true authority.

Which the mistress of the house should perhaps have administered to the muck-crusted 5-year-old bottom of the only daughter, in spite of what she had listened to him say about non-violence.

About the unruffle-able serenity of a "true" master. Early that summer. During an aromatic morning in a row boat on the senator's green-mirroring turtle lake. That had lain in seemingly unruffle-able serenity   dark-brown turtles dropping from the bulrushes like giant bedbugs; ducks & cranes flying crookedly into the morning haze at the almost soundless approach of the row boat.

Until the vehemence of 4¹/₂–year-old boredom finally succeeded in overturning the boat in which it had felt held captive.

The subsequent recounting of which amused the senator to the point of laughter. —One of man's dubious distinctions from other animals. A distinction the senator thought he shared with the gods.— Although he had very nearly lost:

1 & only 4¹/₂–year-old daughter
1 27¹/₂–year-old better-born wife
1 18-year-old well-muscled Teutonic rowing slave
& 1 33-year-old Greek (Spartan) thinking slave in the process.

Whose fault it would have been if all four of them had drowned.

For thinking inadequately.

For not knowing how to capture a 4¹/₂- year-old attention. From the first day the first word on. For capturing & holding the mother's 27¹/₂–year-old attention instead.

For not quite daring to take physically punitive measures. Which were not only not in keeping with his non-violence principles, but also contrary to certain basic considerations of prudence: a slave striking his master's 4¹/₂-5-5¹/₂-6-6¹/₂-etc.-etc.-year-old daughter in the presence of the 27¹/₂–28-etc.-etc.-year-old mother. Who had listened to years of his monologues about the laziness of violence. While he & the mother continued to ignore the growing only daughter's daily growing boredom.

Preferring to praise the excellence of melon marmalade, when the 6¹/₂–year-old flayed an entire field of richly ripe melons which they were passing with a frenzied stick.

When he & the mother continued walking. While he continued to talk. About: "Miniature suns, shining from a deep-green foliage sky." & about: "The recurrence of the egg shape everywhere in nature. The neuter still neutral shape of the fruit/the seed. With its promise of male & female. Before the split into male & female. Into pistil & petals . . ." & about: "The all-pervading elementary trinity of: earth   water   air; recurring in flesh   blood   breath . . . in stem   sap   green . . ." Etc. Etc. Etc. Etc. Etc. Etc. Etc. . . . Rather than use the frenzied stick on the melon-shaped   already blatantly female $6^1/2$– year-old bottom.

A subsequent recounting of which   by the sore-bot- tomed only daughter   might not have amused the senator to the point of gods-shared laughter.

Might, on the contrary, have prompted the not-amused senator to revise his thinking slave's Greek/Spartan tutoring methods by cutting off the slavish hand that had dared strike his master's only daughter. Or   more simply   to cut off the slavish head, in order to put a stop to the kind of thinking that led to slaves striking their master's only daughter.

Whose increasingly violent boredom-tantrums were well in keeping with Roman patrician tradition: according to the sena- tor's Greek/Spartan thinking slave's unrevised thinking.

The same frantic attempts to silence   with screams of childish rage; & later with the screams of victims: of animals/of slaves   the inner voice that was telling them how unfree they were.

Were free perhaps not to listen to their fathers' thinking slaves, but not free to listen to the whisper voice inside them that kept telling them that they   the proud patricians   the empire builders   the history makers   were abject menial slaves. To their needs & greeds. To their craving for effect-producing. For constant worldwide attention.

Were more enslaved than the slaves who served them. Who ruled them, by serving them. Who might some day start ruling them without continuing to serve them, if they continued to ignore their own inner whisper voices. Until they'd become unable to ignore the whisper voices of their slaves.

Who were beginning to question the self-mastery of their masters. In the different idioms of their different ethnic & social backgrounds. Which their enslaved state was melting into one

language, spoken & understood by all. The language of passive
resistance. In echo-response to the suffering inflicted upon most
of them by obesely bored masters. Who called their thoughtless
     or, on the contrary, their minutely thought-out   cruelties:
necessary punitive measures. Healthy discipline. When they
themselves lacked even the discipline not to over-eat. & dieted
by proxy, by starving their slaves . . .

     Who had somehow begun to hear what the senator's
Greek/Spartan thinking slave had been thinking out loud, for 7
or 8 years. In the course of his less & less prudent, more & more
outspoken daily monologues.
     Which they'd begun to repeat to one another. In the dif-
ferent idioms of their different ethnic & social backgrounds.
     Which ceased being monologues, after the suddenly lis-
tening 12^1/$_2$-year-old only daughter began to contradict whatever
she thought she had heard. Vehemently. & to repeat to the senator whatever she thought she had heard that she had contradicted.
     Incorrectly.
     Not understanding whatever it was that he might have
said. Somewhat more prudently, lately. About: The importance
of understanding, for instance. The relative unimportance   the
luxury   of being understood . . .
     About: with all due respects   Juvenal's somewhat
unfortunate statement that *mens sana in corpore sano* was the
greatest gift of the gods.
     Treating mind & body as two separate entities. As though
the mind were not part of the body. As much a part of the body
as the hands/the feet. When we needed our whole body to think
with. Could understand a concept only after we'd felt its applications with our body.
     Which was perhaps why Juvenal was so often misunder-
stood. Hygienically misunderstood. Misquoted, as though he had
meant to say that a healthy body was the *conditio sine qua non*
for a healthy mind.

Which made about as much sense as saying that a broken leg prevented a man from seeing.

Although it might conceivably prevent him from seeing things in places where his broken leg prevented him from going.

Which made the now 14-year-old   now listening only daughter laugh.

Before   or perhaps after   it occurred to her to burn the soles of one of her father's slave girl's feet with hot stones which she'd ordered the girl to heat, in order to understand the concept of pain.

Which made the senator share in the laughter of his only daughter   which both shared with the gods   after she described to him what she had done after what the thinking slave had said.

Which the now listening only daughter had perhaps willfully misunderstood.

Perhaps she was making a game of misunderstanding.

A game in which the senator was perhaps sharing, when he repeated to all of Rome what his Greek/Spartan thinking slave had *not* said.

For every potentially rebellious slave to hear. & to repeat.

To make them believe that he had actually said: No man is truly free until he has a slave. After he'd been given his freedom. & a slave of his own.

Whom to set free he was not free enough.

Nor was he free enough to leave Rome & return to Sparta.

He was free only to continue living in the small crude house on his former master's grounds in which he had lived for nearly twelve years.

Which felt smaller now that he had to share it with his slave. A not-overly-bright, not-overly-clean girl from southern Gaul whom enslavement had aged prematurely. Sullenly.

Who sullenly practiced   on him   the passive resistance he had preached.

Who felt further degraded by serving a former slave. A

former "equal." Whom she mistrusted, because she'd been told
what he had not said, after he'd been given his freedom. Which
he had no way of rectifying, since she spoke neither Greek nor
the language of Rome.

Hardly spoke   or washed   at all. A sullen   slightly
smelly   presence. That he felt the unexpected temptation to
beat, at times, when she kept persistently in his way, in the
smaller-seeming crude house.

Which he no longer had any reason   or excuse   to
leave. Since the senator had deemed that his only daughter was
well able to think like a man   like a true Roman   at 16;
almost $16^{1}/_{2}$. & that his 45-year-old Greek/Spartan former thinking slave therefore had no further need to think out loud. In the
listening almost daily presence of the almost $39^{1}/_{2}$–year-old
yet barely perceptibly; serenely   aging mother.

Who had sent the Spartan/Greek former thinking slave the
jug of wine he had just finished drinking.

The dregs of which had the color & texture of slowly
drying blood.